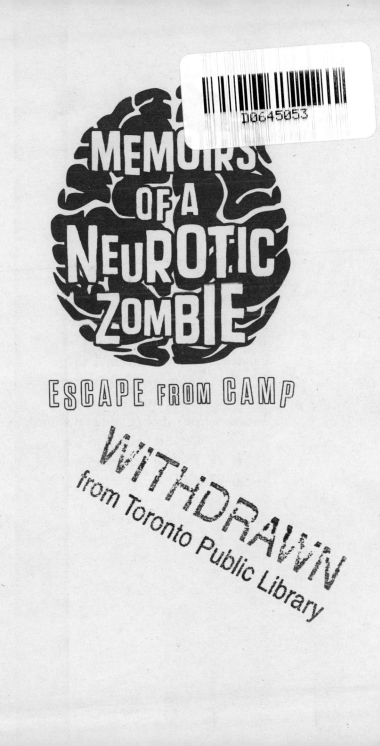

MEMOIRS OF A NeuROTIC ZOMBIE

ESCAPE FROM CAMP

FABER & FABER

has published children's books since 1929. Some of our very first publications included *Old Possum's Book of Practical Cats* by T. S. Eliot, starring the now world-famous Macavity, and *The Iron Man* by Ted Hughes. Our catalogue at the time said that 'it is by reading such books that children learn the difference between the shoddy and the genuine'. We still believe in the power of reading to transform children's lives.

About the author

Jeff took a long time to become an author. He grew up in Canada, worked in America, and now lives in London with his wife and two sons.

Before writing stories for a living, Jeff did lots of other jobs, including delivering newspapers, cleaning toilets, caddying at bridge (the card game) tournaments, umpiring baseball games, ushering at the local cinema, driving executives around, devising business plans, developing new products, marketing washing-up liquid, pushing a mail cart, reading scripts, making movies, running the Enid Blyton literary estate, and developing and producing TV shows.

With perhaps the exception of ushering at the cinema, writing is his favourite job.

When he's not dreaming up stories and writing them down, Jeff is on the web at www.jeffnorton.com and on social media as @thejeffnorton.

By the same author

Memoirs of a Neurotic Zombie

The MetaWars series

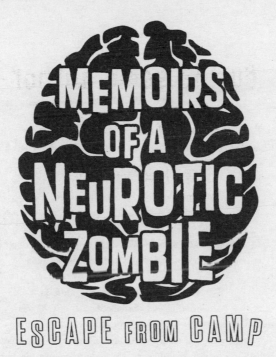

MEMOIRS OF A NEUROTIC ZOMBIE

ESCAPE FROM CAMP

JEFF NORTON

ff

FABER & FABER

First published in 2015
by Faber & Faber Limited
Bloomsbury House,
74–77 Great Russell Street,
London WC1B 3DA

Typeset by MRules
Printed in England by CPI Group (UK) Ltd, Croydon CR0 4YY

A CIP record for this book
is available from the British Library

ISBN 978–0–571–31188–0

FSC
www.fsc.org
MIX
Paper from
responsible sources
FSC® C101712

2 4 6 8 10 9 7 5 3 1

For Mom & Dad . . .
. . . who *never* rented out my room.

1

In Which I Say Goodbye to Seventh Grade

It was the last day of seventh grade and everyone at school was excited for summer, except for me.

I've always preferred the structure of school to the chaos of summer. Besides being hot and sticky, July and August are family road-trip months. Each year, Dad piles us into the minivan and hurls us down a potholed interstate for enforced family fun. But he's more focused on 'making good time' than having a good time. To be honest, it's misery on wheels. Mom frets about her patients, Amanda stays glued to her phone, and I get carsick.

Every time.

Cramming four humans (well, three humans plus a zombie) in a steel cage and hurtling down the highway at sixty-five miles per hour is not a recipe for anything but family friction, body odour, and vomit.

And besides, since coming back from the dead, I just don't have that much in common with my family unit any more. They're the living, and I'm ... the living dead.

When you're a zombie, you don't fit in like you used to.[*]

At school, I just do my best to blend in. Thanks to all the make-up tips I found on YouTube, I now cover up my decomposing, grey skin. It may not look supple and vibrant, but at least it passes for tweenage and pubescent. And since I'd lied about faking my own death to hide out in the Witness Relocation Programme, Croxton Middle School welcomed me back as a pupil. Nobody except my family and two new best friends, Ernesto the cheeky chupacabra and Corina the vegan vampire, needed to know that death had actually relocated me to a dark grave for three months.

It felt good to be back in seventh grade, but now it was coming to a close – the last day of school.

'It all goes home or in the garbage,' shouted Mr Paulson, our gym teacher. He marched up and down the hallway,

---

[*] Yep, you heard me right. I am a zombie. If you're coming to this story without knowing that, I suggest you track down a copy of my first book, *Memoirs of a Neurotic Zombie*.

ordering us soon-to-be eighth graders to empty our lockers before his summer could start. I carefully cleaned out my locker, which was not only my depot for hand sanitisers (I just didn't trust the soap in the boy's room), but also my shrine to the best superhero of all time.

But not even NinjaMan could save me from the annual summer road trip.

As I delicately packed up my belongings (everything in its place!), I wondered where Dad would hijack us to this summer. He was obsessed with the Founding Fathers[*], so I made a bet with Amanda that we'd schlep to Boston or Washington; maybe Philly if we were unlucky. Amanda's money was on Montana, convinced it was the one state in the union that didn't have reliable 3G coverage – thus cutting her off from the Croxton social scene for a season.

'A fate worse than death!' she'd declared at breakfast. 'Oh, sorry Adam,' she added hastily. 'But in the summer before high school, I've got to be available, accessible, and noticed.'

---

[*] My mother liked to remind him that America's founding 'fathers' simply signed a break-up letter to the King of England stating, 'It's not you, it's me,' and then fought a war about it. 'Hardly an example of good fatherhood,' she says.

As I carefully peeled the limited edition NinjaMan v Amphibulus poster off my locker door, I detected a slight whiff of grapefruit and toilet cleaner in the air. It instantly made me smile.

'Hey zom-boy, can I talk to you?'

I inhaled Corina's familiar (and comforting) scent of SPF 150 – 'the strongest sun protection a vampire could buy'. She was clad in black, like she'd just stepped off a goth runway.*

'You mean like ... out loud?' I checked. 'At school, in front of other people?'

'Yeah, well.' She shrugged. 'Last day of school and all that – thought I'd make an exception.'

Sure we were friends. Sure we fought evil together. Sure I had a massive, unrequited† crush on her. But Corina Parker was something else. She was a vegan.‡

A vegan vampire.§

But despite worshipping Count Dracula, Corina had

---

* The kind used by beautiful models, not aeroplanes. Though her scent did have an intoxicating top note of jet fuel. Man, she was awesome!

† Unrequited, as in not returned. I liked her, like, a lot, and I think she tolerated me.

‡ A vegan is someone who doesn't eat any meat or anything that comes from an animal, so no dairy, milk, butter, or eggs.

§ And also generally no bloodsucking.

4

rejected her kind's ancient bloodsucking tradition. She avoided touching anything that comes from an animal (or person) with the notable exception of her very expensive leather jacket.

And since she never talked to me at school, I knew something was wrong.

'Did you get too much sun exposure today?' I asked.

I rummaged on the top shelf in the basket carefully labelled 'Outer Wear' for a wide-brimmed sun hat. Before dying I had very sensitive skin and always took protective measures. But one good thing about being dead is that skin cancer can't develop on dead skin. It's one of the few benefits to being a zombie.

'I don't need your hat or your charity,' she snapped.

'Is it a woman thing?' I whispered.

'Seriously?' she barked. 'Is that your assumption for *everything*?'

It really wasn't, but it's a shortcut I probably use too often. I don't understand girls. Females are a confusing species and by definition everything about them is a 'woman thing'. But this was something more. Something was troubling Corina.

'Fine,' she snapped. 'I just needed a friend and clearly knocked on the wrong door.'

'You didn't *even* knock,' I said.

She stomped off down the hall, the steel spikes of her black boots announcing her exit as she *click-clanked* away.

'Wait, Corina!' I called after her, abandoning my open locker.

'Meltzer,' called Mr Paulson, stepping in front of me. 'Is your locker vacated and ready for summer?'

I looked back. It wasn't. It was still midway through a very careful deconstruction. I had NinjaMan magnets to pack into bubble wrap, coloured pencils to put in order from lightest to darkest, and a set of spare clothes to remove and fold properly.

In truth, I was just getting started.

'Whatever's left in your locker feeds the landfill,' he warned.

I looked past the beefy gym teacher, which wasn't easy, to see Corina disappear around the corner towards the sixth-grade wing. She was clearly upset and, as she said, needed a friend.

All of my instincts were telling me to back up and pack up. I had cherished possessions in that locker, things that got me through the past few weeks of my re-entry into Croxton Middle School. But as much as I wanted – no, needed – to clean it out properly, Corina needed me more.

I took one last look at my locker. 'You can junk it all.' I sighed. 'I gotta go.'

'Good man, Meltzer,' he said. 'Don't live in the past.'

I slipped around Mr Paulson and ran down the hallway, dodging the overflowing garbage cans and chattering seventh graders.

As I rounded the corner, I stopped and scanned the corridor of sixth graders. I spotted Ernesto, my backyard neighbour and Croxton's secret chupacabra.[*]

At school, Ernesto Ortega looked like a messy-haired Mexican who uses his sleeves as napkins, but underneath ... he was a monster. He really wanted to be a werewolf but instead he was stuck as a hairless lizard-type creature with huge fangs and bulging black spheres for eyes.

Just then, human Nesto was eyeing something in his

---

[*] If you don't know what a chupacabra is, then what are you doing reading this sequel before you've read my first autobiography? If you've just forgotten, then see a doctor about memory loss, but I'll fill you in: chup-a-ca-bra is a scaly, lizard-like monster that comes out at night and eats rodents and destroys gardens. Like a werewolf but not as wolfy.

locker. He pulled out a mushy brown ball and held it up like a treasure.

'Nesto!' I shouted. 'Did you see Corina?'

'This apple's still good, right?' he asked. A worm oozed out of the skin as if to lay claim to the decayed fruit.

I pointed to the repulsive creature as a warning, but Nesto took it as an invitation.

'Lucky me,' he said, popping the entire bad apple into his mouth.

I looked away, disgusted, and scanned the hallway. Luckily the shrimpy sixth graders were a lot shorter than us in seventh grade and I spotted Corina's black bob at the end of the hall.

'C'mon,' I said. 'Something's wrong with Corina.'

Nesto and I ran to the end of the hallway where the corridor ended at the stage entrance to the auditorium. She was gone. But then I noticed the trapdoor in the ceiling was slightly open.

'The roof,' I said.

'Lift me up,' said Ernesto.

I looked down at his sneakers.

'Is that crusted-on poo?' I asked. 'Maybe you should lift me up.'

'You're bigger,' he said.

'Yes, I'm well fed on a diet that doesn't include worms.'

He growl-hissed at me. For a moment I thought he was about to transmutate into his lizard-like chupacabra alter ego. 'I need the protein, okay?'

'Okay, fine,' I relented. Nesto needed a steady supply of protein the way I needed a bottomless bottle of hand sanitiser. I cupped my hands together and Nesto stepped into them with his non-poo sneaker.

'Now lift me up,' he said. 'Whee!'

Nesto pulled on the door in the ceiling and a steep set of steps slid down.

He clambered up the steps, beckoning me to follow. I paused to consider whether to wash my hands.

But then I heard crying. It was Corina. She was sobbing upstairs and, for the first time in my life, I decided there was just no time for hygiene.

I climbed up the steps and out through another door to emerge onto the flat gravel roof. Corina sat with her legs dangling off the building, sniffling and sobbing all alone.

Nesto stood tentatively beside me, shifting awkwardly on the gravel-topped roof.

'Is it a woman thing?' he asked.

'Really? Is that your assumption for *everything*?' I huffed. 'Um, Corina,' I called, walking slowly towards the edge. 'Are you all right?'

'I'm hungry,' she sobbed.

'Me too,' said Nesto. 'You guys want to come over for quesadilla after school?'

'Not that kind of hungry,' she said.

'Nesto, the processed-cheese food product your mom uses, technically comes from an animal,' I said, 'and you know Corina's a vegan.'

Ernesto shrugged. 'You can just have plain tortilla if you want.'

'You guys don't understand,' she said, wiping the tears from her eyes. 'It's a different hunger, an *ancient* one.'

A few weeks ago, Corina had secretly slipped into the vampire stereotype and sucked human blood. So when she said she was hungry, I guessed it wasn't the kind of hunger that a Snickers could satisfy.

'You mean *vampire* hungry?' I asked. 'Don't you?'

She nodded slowly, as if she was ashamed. 'I need to feed.'

When I'd accidentally crushed* a guy called Crash to death, Corina stepped up so I wasn't guilty of murder. And by 'stepped up' I mean she actually bit into him, sucked his blood and turned him into a vampire.

That was a really big deal for her, and not just because she didn't administer a blood test before actually sucking his blood (which I must advise the reader to never, ever, ever try at home), but because she'd broken her ban.

Corina had joked a few times that she now had a taste for human blood, but was content to eat Pop Rocks† as her main foodstuff. Maybe she hadn't been joking.

I wondered if she could satisfy her hunger with animal protein. 'I know you're vegan, Corina, but animals are really tasty.'

'And legal,' added Nesto.

She shook her head. 'Being down there, in that hallway with all of those kids, I wanted to feed on them. I *needed* to feed.'

---

* Technically, Corina had pushed me, but this didn't feel like the time or place to bring up technicalities.

† Fizzy candy that goes pop in your mouth. The best!

Nesto took a fearful step back, clearly reconsidering his earlier invitation. 'Um,' he uttered, 'you know what, I didn't tell my mom about having anyone over after school. So probably best that we don't do snacks. 'Kay?'

Corina stood up, toes inching over the edge, and looked out across Croxton. The town was dominated by the spires of the university to the north and surrounded by cornfields as far as we could see. It was an island of academia in a sea of newly planted corn.

'This town's full of people, but all I see is food.'

I didn't want my best friend to become a mass murderer, or even worse, a bloodsucking cliché.

'Step away from the ledge,' interrupted a loud, tinny voice. It was the school principal, Mr Eriksen, standing below us and shouting into a megaphone. 'We've called your parents and it's all going to be okay.'

'You called my parents?' gasped Corina.

Mr Eriksen nodded proudly, forcing a big smile across his pale Swedish face.

Corina sighed and slapped her head into her hands. 'Then it's far from okay.'

2

In Which I Choose Life

It turns out that nothing gets townspeople mobilised faster than tweenage despair. Within minutes of Mr Erik Eriksen's uninspiring rallying cry not to jump off the roof ('It's going to be okay,' was the best he could do), the fire department, police department, parks and recreation department, and two television crews turned up to join the throngs of students below who split into two choral camps chanting either, 'jump, jump', or 'don't jump'.

I even spotted a guy selling hot dogs.

Our suspected suicide attempt was quickly becoming a carnival. I noticed my annoying sister Amanda stride towards the principal. She wrestled the megaphone from his oversized hands.

'Adam Meltzer,' she called. 'This stunt will not get you your room back.'

Upon my death, in a period of mourning, Amanda had seen it fit to move into my newly vacated bedroom. The bedroom, I might add, with a bigger closet and two windows facing the front, from where she could spy on who was walking to and from school with whom. She still hadn't given it back and I had to sleep in the basement.

'Ms Meltzer, I think your brother needs your kindness and support right now,' I heard the principal say, snatching the megaphone back.

'He's never had it before,' Amanda said. 'If I give it to him now, he's bound to jump just out of sheer confusion. No, we need to treat these middle-schoolers like the infants they are.'

'Hey!' I called. 'You're not even in high school yet!' *Gawd.*

Amanda always had a superiority complex. But ever since the truck carrying the school's test scores crashed into the mighty Ohio River, giving all the seniors an automatic B+, she marches around town like she owns the place because she is guaranteed to graduate.

But she was marching in a parade of her own self-delusion.

I'd seen enough high school TV shows to know that come September, Amanda will walk through the security arch of Croxton High School and be a goldfish in a shark tank. And then who'd be laughing?

Probably the sharks.

If they could laugh – there is no evidence to suggest they could, but it'd be pretty cool to see a laughing shark.*

Especially after it ate my sister.

But for now, she was annoying me and embarrassing herself . . . on television. One of the TV crews shoved a camera in her face and the local newscaster, Gideon Gilgacrest, put his arm around her.

'I'm here with the sister of the soon-to-be-deceased—' he began.

'Ha!' she laughed (like a shark might). 'He's already dead.'

'Amanda!' I shouted. Shaking my head. I did not want to be outed as a zombie on Channel 7 *News At Nine*.

If I was ever going to come clean about my state of undeadness, I'd want to be on a nationally televised talk show with at least a twenty rating.

---

* Sharks don't actually laugh. But in NinjaMan issue #1193, NinjaMan in the Sharkstorm, they sure did. And it was pretty cool.

Jeez, what do you take me for!

The newscaster continued fabricating the news. '. . . who is clearly distraught about her brother's final moments. Grief, dear, works in mysterious ways.'

'Can you make me famous?' I heard Amanda ask.

Beside me, Corina sat back down, clearly bored by the media circus.

I joined her, dangling my legs off the ledge. It was surprisingly freeing to have nothing but thirty feet of air under your feet. 'I see why you like it up here.'

Nesto settled in on my left, surveying the scene below. 'Yeah, we get a lot of attention. Think they could fling me a hot dog up here?'

'That worm didn't fill you up?' I asked.

'Unwanted attention.' Corina sighed. 'Look guys.'

She pointed to the school parking lot. A black hearse drove in, screeching its tyres in full violation of the school board's ten-miles-per-hour campus speed limit.

'Whoa,' said Nesto. 'They really can't wait to bury us.'

'In a matter of speaking,' said Corina. 'That . . . is my mother.'

16

Mrs Parker drove the hearse up on the curb, nearly hitting the gaggle of students and pushing the hot dog vendor out of the way as she flung open the door. Pink wieners spilled all over the tarmac and Nesto called out, 'Ten-second rule!'*

Corina's mother, dressed all in black and wearing a veil that obscured most of her face, snapped open a black parasol. She glided towards the principal and held out her black-gloved hand. For a man descended from Viking stock, Mr Eriksen surrendered surprisingly quickly. He handed over the megaphone and skulked off to the side to lift a hot dog from the ground, still with about three seconds to go before Nesto's ten-second rule expired.

'Fly down here at once!' she screeched.

'Ah, no, no!' called Mr Limpman, our guidance counsellor, who was rushing across the parking lot, heaving his heft as fast as he could.

'Mother,' said Corina. 'Do not make a scene.'

Mrs Parker scanned the hundreds of students, teachers, and emergency service professionals assembled,

* The 'ten-second rule', for how long a piece of food may remain on the floor before becoming inedible, is more like a guideline than a rule. In my view, anything that touches the floor should be off limits.

17

and sarcastically bit back, 'A little too late for that *dar*-ling.'

'Fine,' said Corina.

She flew to her feet and stood with her steel-toed boots lurching over the edge.

The crowd gasped.

'Corina,' I said. 'I think we ought to go back inside.'

'But I'm having fun,' chirped Ernesto.

'C'mon guys,' I urged. 'Let's go before anyone does anything stupid.'

'Like call my mother?' said Corina.

'It could be worse,' I offered, knowing that for Corina Parker it probably was already worse. 'Let's just meet up tonight. My backyard?'

'Yeah, suppose,' Corina said with a huff, stepping back from the ledge. 'But don't expect me to keep supplying you boys with Pop Rocks. You gotta bring your own stash if you want to keep having three-a.m. rendezvous.'*

'Noted,' I said with a nod.

I really did want to keep having three-a.m. meet-ups with Corina Parker, so I made a mental note to find a reliable bulk supplier of fizzy candy.

* It's a fancy French word for 'meet up'.

18

We shuffled back towards the door in the roof and back inside the air-conditioned comfort of publicly funded education.

When we descended the ladder into the hallway, Mr Limpman greeted us with open arms.

He had giant sweat circles under the armpits of his short-sleeved collared shirt.

I'm not going anywhere near those, I thought.

'You made the right choice, kids,' he said. 'And just know that I'm always here for you to tackle any problems you may be facing.'

Just then the school bell rang.

The last school bell of seventh grade.

'But not until after Labor Day,' he added. 'My holidays start now. Have a great summer and remember to choose life.'

We walked outside into the crowd and Corina's mother grabbed her arm and snatched her away.

'You pull a stunt like that,' she snapped, 'and just before the big convention. I'd hoped you'd be mature enough to attend this year, but after that—'

'Adam,' interrupted my sister, 'I'm glad you didn't die.'

And she leaned in, whispering to my ear, '*Again.*'

I was touched by Amanda's sentiment, but mostly curious about what Mrs Parker was talking about.

'Thanks, sis,' I said. 'But you're still in my room.'

'I'm in high school now,' she said with a smile. 'Just four years until college ... then it's all yours.'

3

In Which I Find Myself Homeless

'Your mother and I have some wonderful news,' announced my dad. He looked at mom with a knowing smile. The kitchen table was covered in a white tablecloth and I noticed that instead of IKEA plates, my oddly giddy parents had opted for the good china. Ordinarily, I'd welcome the formal stuff, but tonight I couldn't shake the feeling that something strange was going on.

I glanced at Amanda, whose jaw hung open with a half-eaten stick of red liquorice drooling from her mouth. She rocked ever so slowly back and forth on her chair, gripped in shock. I raised my eyebrows (feeling my grey forehead skin crack – note to self: double up on face moisturiser) to catch her attention. Amanda placed her hand over her tummy and mimed a baby bump.

Now it was my turn to do some jaw dropping. I knew she'd been hoping to fit into high school, but I figured she'd go for cheerleading, not teenage pregnancy.

'Not me, you idiot,' she scoffed. Amanda pointed her half-eaten, habit-forming liquorice at our mother.

I looked at Mom dishing out the veggie lasagne. She was positively glowing. Dad was even looking at her affectionately as he poured golden, bubbling liquid into tall, thin glasses that looked too fancy for anything but . . . oh, no . . .

. . . it was champagne.

As Corina would say: *Oh. My. Count.* They were having a baby!

My afterlife flashed before my eyes – a terrifying future filled with vomit and poo and indentured* babysitting. Amanda actually started to convulse, ever so slightly, but Mom and Dad were too absorbed in pre-baby bliss to notice.

---

* Indentured is like work that's against your will. It usually has nothing to do with dentures. Fun fact: my favourite Founding Father, Benjamin Franklin, was actually indentured as a boy, forced to work for his older brother, though I have no idea if that job included cleaning his dentures.

They had already stopped paying attention to us. My entire world was crumbling around me. I had to take charge of this apocalypse.*

'You can't have a baby!' I declared. 'I'm your baby!'

Dad dropped his champagne. The glass shattered on the china plate and I watched in slow motion as the bubbly liquid doused the tablecloth.

Mom stared at me. It reminded me of the first time she'd seen me in zombie form. There was fear, but there was also love.

'First of all,' she said. 'I'll get some paper towels.' She rose from the table carefully and backed herself up to the kitchen counter. 'Second, you are not a baby. And third, most importantly, I'm not having a baby. I am too busy for a baby.'

But Amanda kept rocking herself back and forth muttering something about life being over.

'You're worrying me, Amanda,' said Dad.

'We're the ones who should be worried,' she said.

'She has a point,' I said, hating to agree with her.

---

* Apocalypse (sounds like: a-pock-a-lips) is a big word that means the end of the world. It's a big thing in the Bible and in pretty much every zombie movie, which tend to be about 'the zombie apocalypse', which survivors tend to think is a bad thing.

'Look at the evidence: tablecloth, Grandma's fine china, champagne, you two making googly eyes at each other. The signs are clear.'

My parents just laughed.

They laughed and laughed ... and laughed.

Mom poured herself a glass of the bubbles and downed it in one gulp.

'No, Adam,' she said with a smile, 'we're celebrating because this summer there's a big convention of dentists coming to town.'

'And they need rooms to stay in,' added my dad. 'So we've rented out your bedrooms.'

'Huh?' grunted Amanda.

'And with the money we'll get,' said Mom with a grin, 'we're sending you kids away to camp.'

'So, no road trip?' I asked.

Dad shook his head. 'We know you kids don't really like the Meltzer family road trip. But camp, wow, you're going to love it!'

This was almost too much to process. In the breath of about one minute, I went from being an uncle, to an older brother, to a refugee from my own home.

'Amanda, dear,' said Mom, mopping up Dad's bubbles with a puff of paper towel. 'Chew your liquorice.'

Dad picked little bits of glass off the table and placed them in what was left of his champagne flute.

'Ouchy,' he yelped, pulling his finger away. 'Cut myself.'

He held up his index finger and blood trickled down his digit.

Knockity-knock-knock.

I looked over at the window and spotted Corina floating outside. Her eyes were wide, fixated on Dad's bloody finger. She licked her lip gloss. I shook my head frantically. I did not want her vamping out on my dad. She landed on her two feet and stood there, waiting. I tried to shoo her away but she didn't move.

'Adam, what are you—?' asked my mom. 'Oh, it's your little friend, Corina.'

'Adam's-got-a-girlfriend,' teased Amanda.

'She's not my girl—'

Then Mom waved her in. 'Come on in, dear, if you don't mind the chaos.'

'Whoa,' I protested. 'You can't *invite* her in.'*

---

* In vampire lore, a vampire must be invited inside in order to enter someone's home. They may be bloodsucking creatures from an ancient evil, but I respect that they have manners.

'Lovers' quarrel?' my sister pestered.

'Don't be rude, Adam,' said my Dad, trying to stem the bleeding by pressing his finger against his lips.

'Are you hungry, dear?' Mom asked, before turning to me. 'She looks too thin to me – do you think she eats enough, Adam?'

I had no idea how to respond to that one.

Corina stepped in through the screen door on the downstairs landing and bounded up with a stricken look on her pale face.

'Don't mind the Meltzers,' said Dad, now sucking his bleeding finger. 'Just a bit of family insanity here.'

Corina stared at Dad's cut. Her mouth gaped opened and I swear her incisors grew.

'Corina was just going home,' I said, rising to escort her out the front door and as far away from my bleeding father as I could.

'I don't have a home any more,' she said.

'What?' I asked.

'My parents gave away my room and even my cof— my cosy bed to my relatives coming to the convention.'

'Lots of dentists in your family then?' asked my dad.

'It's in the blood,' Corina explained.

'We were just telling the kids the good news,'

explained my mom. 'We've rented out their rooms to dentists and with the extortionate* rent we're able to charge, we're sending them away to camp.'

Camp. The very word filled me with fear. A place filled with mosquitos but void of basic plumbing. Like the Dark Ages.

'And they leave tomorrow!' my dad said with a smile.

He raised his new glass of bubbles and clinked glasses with mom, sealing my fate.

'Wait,' I said to Corina, pulling her into the front hallway. 'Did she just say "dentists"?'

'That's what I was coming over to tell you,' Corina whispered, before reinstating normal volume to avoid suspicion. 'About all of the "dentists" coming to town.'

'And by dentists,' I said softly, 'what you really mean is ...'

With her back to my family, she shot me a smile. Her incisors had grown into bloodsucking fangs. Then she closed her mouth to cover up her secret.

'... vampires.'

---

* Extortionate. It means, like, really high, as in expensive. Like the NinjaCave playset (complete with the Nin-jet!) that I told Mom I wanted for my birth (and death) day but that she said was ridiculously extortionate.

4

In Which I Face My Fate

That night, at three in the morning, I woke in the darkness of the basement to the sound of buzzing. It was Adamini, the zombee who'd killed me. But I don't hold a grudge and this pigeon-sized bee had actually become something between a friend and a pet. After all, it wasn't his fault he was the product of an evil science experiment.

He buzzed over my head and nudged me out of my lumpy cot bed. Turns out that genetically modified, death-defying bees are very reliable alarm clocks.

Adamini jumped on my shoulder and I lumbered upstairs to meet up with Nesto and Corina in the backyard. It had become our nightly ritual – a space to be friends, a place to be unnatural. Since my death and unexpected (though not unwelcome) return, I'd come to cherish these night-time hang-outs with the only two 'people' who knew what it felt like to be completely different from their families.

Nesto jumped over the back fence in full chupa mode. His body was lizard-like and slimy. He blinked his big black eyes at me and asked, 'Have you heard the news?'

Now, ever since I'd discovered Croxton's collection of supernatural beings and uncovered an evil plot at the university to turn the townsfolk into zombies, I have to admit that the local 'news', which only seemed to focus on house fires and traffic accidents, held little appeal. But I suspected Nesto was talking about the Great Summer Camp Evacuation.

'I just got back and they're kicking me out,' I said.

'It'll be great,' hissed Ernesto. 'I can't wait to let loose in the wild.'

*

Adamini buzzed into the air and swarmed around Nesto, who jumped around the backyard after the playful zombee.

I glanced up at Corina's house, two doors down, and spotted her floating down to join us.

'I can't believe I'm being cleared out of Croxton,' she complained as she made a perfect landing.

'We all are,' I said.

'Even *my* room's been rented,' Nesto said, 'and you can't even see the floor for all my underwear.'

'Our parents have been bought,' I said with a sigh. 'And they can't wait to get rid of us. Doctor Mom says the bus picks us up first thing in the morning.'

'Mother thinks I'm not mature enough to join the convention,' moaned Corina.

'You actually *want* to be a dentist?' asked Nesto.

Corina recoiled. 'The human mouth disgusts me.'

I loved that we had that in common.

'Nesto,' I explained, 'the dentists are just a front for Corina's kind.'

'Vegans?' he asked.

'Vampires,' she clarified. 'The convention is a gathering of vampires from every country around the world, held every four years—'

'Like the Olympics,' chirped Ernesto, excitedly.

'Just like,' snapped Corina. 'If the Olympics included events like human sacrifice, flying races, competitive coffin building, skull tossing—'

'Not catching?' asked Ernesto. 'That'd be way funner to watch.'

'*Funner* is not a real word,' I clarified.

30

'I don't want to go to their stupid convention anyway,' sulked Corina, but I'm pretty sure she was lying.

'Human sacrifice, really?' I asked.

'I don't really know,' she admitted. 'My dad used to tell me about the conventions as coffin-time stories, but I never really knew what to believe. They probably talk big but just stay up late watching the Twilight movies.'*

Ernesto put a claw on her leather-clad shoulder and said, 'Camp will be great, and we'll all be together. What's funner than that?'

Corina sneered at the chupa claw. 'Do *you* want to be a candidate for human sacrifice?'

'Good thing I'm not human,' he said.

'I'm sure exceptions can be made,' she said.

I motioned to Nesto to remove the claw from her Prada jacket. He slipped his claw off the leather and Corina smiled. 'You're right, Ernesto. At least we'll be together.'

---

* I wasn't sure if this was a form of entertainment or torture.

5

In Which I Catch the Bus of Doom

Morning arrived with the scent of slightly burned pancakes, tempting me upstairs to the land of the living. Adamini was already up, buzzing around the basement and eager to get out and stretch his wings.

I rolled off Lumpy Cot and carefully made my bed, complete with hospital corners (not that I'd ever willingly spend any time in a hospital – they are just full of sick people). Adamini buzzed straight at me, tugging at my NinjaMan PJs. I was pretty sure the bee needed to pee.

I opened the back door on the landing and reminded him to keep a low profile while he did his beesness. He nodded and buzzed off.

I think he understood.

Upstairs, Mom and Dad were sitting at the kitchen table, smiling at one another. Amanda gorged on a triple stack of pancakes topped with red liquorice bits.

'Good morning, camper!' boomed Dad. 'Way to be up and Adam!'

He actually slapped his knee, laughing to himself. The proper phrase is 'up and at 'em'. I think he actually named me Adam just so he'd have a recurring joke.

'Up and Adam.' He giggled to himself again.

'You're all packed and ready to go,' said Mom. It seemed she couldn't wait to get rid of us. She pointed to my clothes neatly folded on my chair.

'I took the liberty,' she said.

'You sure did,' I replied, noticing that my T-shirt was folded vertically, not in my preferred horizontal format.[*]

I grabbed my Mom-approved-outfit (NinjaMan retro tee, boxer briefs, cargo shorts) and rushed upstairs to get showered and changed. After a thorough cleansing, I moisturised and applied the make-up I needed to hide my grey zombie skin.

When I returned downstairs, I spotted two large duffel bags dominating the still newly carpeted front hall. One was marked 'Adam' and the other 'Amanda'.

---

[*] I'm asking for a plastic folding board, like the ones they have at Gap, for Christmas this year, but until then I keep a cardboard replica under my bed.

33

They looked worryingly like canvas coffins. I unzipped my bag to make sure all of the essentials were packed (they were), and stuffed in my trusty PJs.

'What's with the pancakes?' I asked, returning to the kitchen.

'Not the pancakes,' said Mom, pouring brownish golden liquid over her stack. 'The real question is what's with the *syrup*?'

'Real maple syrup,' said Dad with a smile.

'I'll pass on the tree secretion,' I said.

Amanda shook her head at me. 'Trees don't have secrets, stupid.'

'*Canadian* maple syrup,' Dad added. 'And why are we not buying American, you might want to know?'

'Just load it on,' ordered Amanda. 'Don't care where it comes from.'

Mom leaned in. 'Adam, Amanda, your camp is in Canada. Isn't that exciting?'

'So eat up, *eh*!' said Dad with a smile.

'That's a foreign country,' I said.

'You can't send us there,' Amanda protested. 'I doubt they even have the Internet in their igloos. And I cannot be out of touch.'

'We've got good news for you dear on both fronts,'

said Dad. 'You'll be in tents, not igloos, and a bunch of us parents got together and loads of the kids from Croxton are going to Camp Nowannakidda as well.'

'So you can keep all your cliques intact,' said Mom.

'You'll love it there, kids.' Dad beamed. 'The camp owner, a really nice old lady, came to town and she gave a big presentation. It looks like so much fun. Oh, to be a kid again.'

'She showed a slide show of the campers swimming, playing sports, singing around campfires, and doing talent shows,' Mom explained.

'And eating doughnuts,' added my dad. 'She brought some – they're amazing!'

He closed his eyes and licked his lips. 'I can still taste them.'

'Your father ate *three*,' my Mom said, 'because he's clearly not worried about his resting metabolic rate.'

'Speaking of eating,' I said. 'I think they have bears up there. Polar, grizzly – you know, the kind that eats kids.'

'I'm sure it's very safe, Adam,' Doctor Mom said. 'Besides, we've paid the money, signed all the release forms . . .'

'Release from what?'

Mom and Dad looked at one another.

'It's fine print stuff, champ. Grown-up stuff. Blah-blah,

not our fault if you get eaten by a bear, that kind of thing.'

'Not funny Dad,' I said. 'There's a reason we live in cities and houses and not in the wild. The wild is wildly unpredictable!'

'Come on you two,' urged my mom. 'The bus leaves soon, so eat up!'

Amanda faked a bear impression as she devoured her pancakes.

'And our new tenants arrive this afternoon.' Dad smiled, rubbing his hands together in anticipation of the small fortune the vampire dentists would pay to take over our home. 'Your mother and I are doing a road trip, just the two of us.'

'Just like our honeymoon,' Mom said.

I couldn't believe how eager they were to get rid of us.

Mom and Dad walked to the bottom of the street and we joined a gaggle of parents and kids saying their goodbyes. I spotted Nesto and Corina. Jake was there too and at least a quarter of my soon-to-be eighth-grade class.* It seemed the Croxton parents were really cashing in on the vampire influx.

* Jake is probably my best human friend and we go to the comics store together every Wednesday.

36

I waved to Nesto, who was surrounded by his siblings and enveloped in a smothering hug from both his mom and his grandma. He wriggled out leaving his elders to continue their embrace. Nesto's mom was weeping and I wasn't sure if it was from joy or despair.

Then I found Corina in the crowd, all alone. I moved to tap her on the shoulder and remembered the no touching rule.

'Your parents aren't into family send-offs?' I asked.

'They're busy, you know with the *dentist* convention.'

'Hey, Adam,' said Jake, clutching an orange plastic bag from Croxton Hardware and Comics. 'Yo, Corina.'

She stared at him. 'Never *yo* me!'

'Guess what's in the bag,' Jake said excitedly.

'Let me take a wild guess,' said Corina. 'Not hardware.'

'I stocked up for the summer,' he said, revealing a stack of graphic novels. 'I don't think they have comic shops in the wilderness.'

A big bus rounded the corner and musically honked its horn. It sounded like a war cry from a tribal drumbeat. The destination sign announced 'No Stop Till Nowannakidda', and as the bus stopped, its door hissed open, a grinning camp director leaned out and invited us to: 'Climb on for a one-way ticket to summer fun!'

He introduced himself as Gordon, but claimed his camp name was 'Growl', which he said while embarrassingly impersonating a bear.

Growl wore cargo shorts, an open plaid shirt over a white T-shirt and a sweat-stained baseball cap over his flowing, golden hair. He looked like a twenty-something surfer who'd been kicked off the waves one too many times.

'All aboard, kids!' he called. 'I've got a checklist and I intend to check it. And parental types, give your kids one last squeeze. It's camp time for them!'

He called off our names one by one, and each of us, except for Corina, gave our parents a goodbye hug.

Once everyone was aboard and settled in surprisingly clean and comfortable seats (with seat belts I might add!), the bus driver, a grim, gaunt-looking man, started the engine.

I grabbed a seat beside Corina, right behind Nesto.

She twitched when the door closed. 'I don't think this is a good idea, Adam.'

Thirty human kids were locked inside a steel bus with one hungry vampire.

She licked her lips and I whispered into her ear, 'Be strong, Corina.'

Corina smiled. 'You're a good friend, Adam.'

Growl announced that the trip would take about ten hours – four hours to the border and then another six or so to reach the woods where Camp Nowannakidda was nestled in 'an ancient native forest filled with wonder and excitement'.

'And mosquitos?' I asked.

'Oh yeah,' he said with bizarre enthusiasm. 'There's a lot of bloodsucking at Camp Nowannakidda.'

'They have no idea,' said Corina, pinching her nose.

I shook my head at Corina. 'Just keep the cravings at bay.'

'I'm doing my best,' she said with a nasal voice that made her sound a bit like a cartoon character. But since I valued our friendship and my limbs intact, I wasn't ever going to tell her that. She unpinched her nose and took a big breath in. 'I can smell the blood moving though everyone on this bus. Well, not you, Adam, and not Ernesto because he mostly smells of must and rotten roadkill.'

'Did you say roadkill?' Nesto asked, turning around. He was sitting in the seats in front of us. 'Hey, have either of you guys ever been to camp before?'

Both Corina and I shook our heads.

'This is the first summer when I haven't been forced on a Meltzer family road trip.'

'My parents haven't exactly encouraged mingling with the masses,' Corina said. 'When we visited my relatives in Transylvania last summer, Mom sent me off to a sort of summertime finishing school with "our kind" and I suppose that was like camp for vampires. We mostly learned how to be snooty and aloof.'

I caught Ernesto's eyes widen. We were both thinking the same thing: *that explains a lot.*

'What?' Corina snapped, seeing our silent understanding.

'I'm excited about the food,' said Nesto.

'Somehow,' I said, 'I don't think camp catering is going to be our finest meals.'

'Nah,' Ernesto laughed. 'I'm excited for the *wild* food. I'm thinking moose, beaver, deer, maybe even a bear. A chupa can't live on squished squirrels forever, Adam. It isn't natural.'

'I honestly don't know whether to be impressed with your optimism or disgusted by your appetite.'

'Why not both?' he chirped.

Corina sighed. 'I suppose they'll have nothing vegan. Good thing I packed a duffel bag full of candy.'

'Apparently there'll be doughnuts,' I said.

'Now you're talking, zom-boy.'

'My mom ate, like, ten at the presentation,' said Ernesto. 'She said they were to die for.'

6

In Which We Invade Canada

The bus trundled north as the flat Ohio landscape breezed by. Eventually we hit Detroit and stopped at the Canadian border. Two uniformed guards, a moustached man and a scowling woman, climbed aboard to inspect us.

'Welcome to Canada,' said the man. 'What's the purpose of your visit?'

Growl spoke up. 'These lucky kids have got a summer of fun, activities, and adventure ahead of them at Camp Nowannakidda.'

'All right,' said the woman, 'we'll just check your passports and you can be on your way.'

'Hand 'em forward,' demanded Growl. 'Come on, campers! Adventure awaits!'

Everyone passed up their blue passports and Growl shared the stack with the border officers. The moustached man strode down the aisle to check me out. He looked at my passport photo, which was just over a year old.

'New with the make-up, kid?' he asked.

'It's a phase,' I said.

'Just lay off the perfume up north,' he cautioned. 'It'll attract the bears.'

I wasn't thrilled about someone else holding on to my passport, but right then my anxiety turned to the bears.

I just hoped that Nesto's chupacabra could keep the bears away.

It wasn't long before we were on the open Canadian road, a highway surrounded by cornfields. I noticed a sign for a rest stop up ahead and asked Growl if we could stretch our legs and get some fresh air.

The bus driver mumbled something about tanking up and Growl agreed to pull us over at the next service station.

As we pulled in, I noticed a giant, golden doughnut on a pole. In neon lettering, it read: Can Nibble Donuts!

'Doughnut run!' announced Nesto.

'Do you know what's in those?' I asked.

'I'm with chuppy,' said Corina. 'I'm starving and after four hours in the tank with the scent of blood, I'm dying for a doughnut.'

Growl led everyone off the bus and they lined up to spend their dough on fried dough. I joined Nesto and Corina as they approached the counter of the doughnut seller. I spotted a sign that asked: 'Can Nibble? Yes you can!' It proudly declared that the Can Nibble Donut Corporation had over two thousand shops serving the doughnut needs of Canadians from coast to coast.

'Can I help you?' asked the lady behind the counter.

'I'll pass,' I said.

'Watching your figure?' she asked.

Nesto laughed. 'I'll have a Cruel Summer Cruller, a Sunrise Sprinkle, and a Chocolate Concoction.'

'I'll take a party pack of Can Nibblers,' said Corina, pointing to the sign above the counter. The Can Nibblers were little doughnut holes with faces painted on them. They looked overly happy given they were about to be eaten, digested, and eventually excreted.

'A party pack is just twelve Nibblers,' the lady replied. 'You'll save more with a two-four.'

Nesto pushed his cruller into his face and nearly cried with glee. 'Thishishamazang,' he mumbled.

'Sold,' said Corina, handing over the money.

The woman looked at the American dollars and smiled. 'Hope you enjoy our national delicacy.'

Corina grabbed a little Nibbler, smiled back at its little icing smile, and popped it into her mouth.

'Oh My Count,' she nearly screamed. 'Nesto's right. A-maze-zing!'

She quickly grabbed three more of her two-four and swallowed those doughnut holes, well, whole. I swear she purred. She stood a little taller and I think her skin almost glowed.

'Those are weally good,' she said, with her mouth full.

The doughnut pusher smiled. 'I know the feelin' honey.'

Growl swaggered up behind us with a big grin on his tanned face. 'You guys've discovered our delicacy, eh?'

'Sogrood,' chomped Nesto.

'I'll take a dozen Icing Igloos, and a dozen Northern Lights,' he ordered, noticing I wasn't stuffing my face. 'Adam, you're not partaking?'

I shook my head.

'Watching my figure,' I joked.

'We'll fatten you up at camp,' he said. 'The food rocks and there's plenty of it.'

'I like my BMI* where it is,' I said.

---

* BMI stands for body mass index. It's an important calculation to see if you're over or under weight. I need to check if there's such a thing as a ZMI, zombie mass index.

'Adam,' he said, 'like a great philosopher once said: you gotta *live* while you're alive.'

'What philosopher?' I asked.

'Jon Bon Jovi,' he said.

'Okay,' I relented, if only to avoid getting life lessons from old rock stars. 'I'll have one bite.'

Corina offered me a little Nibbler – a dark brown ball encased in pearlescent icing. I bit into the soft, sugary dough. It was like biting off a piece of heaven.[*]

The sugar coated my tongue like a properly made bed. The dough was denser than I'd expected, but somehow not heavy. As I chewed, the jam inside oozed out, bursting into my mouth like I'd cracked a piñata of pure pleasure.

'A two-four, please!' I immediately ordered.

The server smiled. 'Another Can-Nibble convert,' she said, sharing a grin with Growl.

'Welcome to Canada, kids,' he said. 'I think you're gonna like it up here.'

[*] Not that I've been – as far as I can remember.

7

In Which We Go into the Woods

There's a song called 'The Wheels on the Bus', which melodically recounts all of the various activities that occur on a bus as it drives 'all day long'. As the wheels on our bus went 'round and round', pushing ever northwards, an accurate version of the ditty would go something like:

> *The wheels on the bus go round and round,*
> *Round and round,*
> *Round and round.*
> *The wheels on the bus go round and round, all*
>   *day long.*
> *The chupacabra on the bus goes totally stir-crazy,*
> *Crazy stir-crazy,*
> *Crazy stir-crazy and annoys everyone else on the*
>   *bus.*
> *The vampire on the bus fights her cravings . . .*

The sister on the bus says, 'where's my signal?'
Jake on the bus holds a fart contest . . .
And the zombie on the bus wishes he was back in
the grave.

Eventually we turned off the paved road, trundled down a long dirt road and arrived at a set of tall, barbed gates. I also noticed a couple of watchtowers. Everyone else had passed out from either exhaustion or the dangerously high levels of fart particles in the oxygen supply.* No one else was awake to wonder what the camp was trying to keep out.

'Um, Growl?' I said. 'Why is the camp behind such a big fence?'

'Bears, man,' he said. 'There's bears in these woods and we wouldn't want any of you getting eaten . . . you know, by bears.'

'Makes sense,' I said with an approving nod. For the first time since I'd heard about camp, things were looking up. Here's a place that took safety and security as seriously as I did.

---

* Government health warnings suggest that a concentration of fart particles in the atomosphere of more than 350 parts per million will lead to global smelling.

As we drove through the forested campground, I spotted baseball diamonds carved out of the woods, and a long stretch of waterfront. The water sparkled in the early evening sun. Kids jumped off the dock and splashed around in the water. They looked sun-kissed and happy, completely oblivious to the harmful effects of the sun's UV spectrum and the waterborne parasites they were frolicking amongst. I suppose ignorance truly was a form of bliss.

Corina was eating in her sleep and I noticed her fangs had grown as she dreamt. I nudged her awake.

'We're here,' I said.

She snapped at my hand.

'Easy, tiger,' I said. 'And my, what big teeth you have.'

She touched her enlarged incisors and looked around to see if anyone had noticed. Her fangs retracted. She contorted herself left and right in obvious discomfort.

'Agh,' she groaned. 'My back is aching. I can't believe I'm saying this, but I really miss my coffin.'

After ten hours locked in the mobile fart hothouse, I knew what she meant. 'Maybe you can construct one in arts and crafts,' I said.

She rolled her eyes then pinched her nose. 'Why does it smell so bad in here?'

49

Nesto popped his head over the seats. 'Hey guys.'

'Oh, right,' Corina said. 'We're travelling with the boy who refuses to bathe.'

Nesto did stink so I let him passively take the blame for the smelly situation. I didn't think it was wise or polite to alert Corina to the source of the toxicity.[*]

'Did you see the lake?' asked Nesto. 'I'm totally taking the chupa for a swim tonight.'

'We may be away from Croxton,' I cautioned, 'but let's keep our weirdness to ourselves. We don't want to arouse suspicion.'

'Aren't you tired of hiding, Adam?' asked Corina.

'You're the one who said people were afraid of different,' I said. It was a chore to make myself up every morning to look vaguely human, and I did sometimes fantasise about living out in the open as a zombie. But the world, or at the very least our little corner of it, didn't quite seem ready for the undead, let alone a vegan vampire or tweenage chupacabra.

I remember how upset Corina was with me when I

---

[*] It's pronounced Tox-Sis-City, not Toxi-City, which would be a really cool name for a city in NinjaMan comics. I might write to the publisher on that. Wait, don't steal my idea!

first decided to go back to school. She made me promise not to reveal my undead nature, for fear of being discovered and dissected.

'I think that's what this year's vampire convention is all about,' she told us. 'Our kind is growing tired of living in the shadows of humanity. They want their time in the, well, not so much sun for obvious reasons, but in the spotlight at least.'

As a guy who yearned for Broadway fame but was always relegated to the lip-synching chorus, I could kind of feel for the vampires.

'I just wanna run free,' said Nesto. 'I think I can do that here.'

'Sure,' I said, 'under the cover of darkness, though.'

'Maybe one day we won't need to hide who we are,' pondered Corina.

'Maybe,' I said, trying to be supportive. 'But probably not today, or the next day, or the day after—'

'I get it,' she interrupted.

'Okay campers!' called Growl. 'Time to get your summer on! I'll show you your tents and then we have a big dinner to welcome you and say farewell to the departing campers. Then, and this is awesome, they'll put on their big talent show! Welcome to the Camp

Nowannakidda experience. I want you to enjoy this summer like it's your last! C'mon!'

Another camp counsellor, who was really tanned in a sleeveless T-shirt and ripped jeans, helped us unload our gear from under the bus.

'Name's Duke,' he said with a smile, 'and I'm here to help.'

Growl high-fived his fellow counsellor and then led us into the fields to show us our tents.

Rows of beige canvas triangles were arranged in a grassy field at the edge of the evergreen forest. I was paired with Nesto, and worried that he might transmutate in his sleep. On the girls' side of the field, poor Corina got saddled with Amanda. Jake got a tent to himself because apparently his parents paid extra, but I think it was probably because the camp was concerned about the legal liability putting someone in a closed environment with the foulest farter in the Midwest.

We were assigned an LIT, a 'Leader in Training'. Our LIT was a bubbly girl who looked like she was in high school. Her name was Petal and she had long brown hair tied in a braid. She wore short ripped shorts and a white, red-rimmed T-shirt that read: Camp Nowannakidda! No Kiddin'!

'Yippy day, campers,' she exclaimed. 'I'll give you a few minutes to get settled in, then bring you over for dinner in the mess hall. Later, campfire and ghost stories, maybe a midnight swim if you feel up for it. Any questions?'

I raised my hand.

'Yes, you can wear make-up here,' she said. 'We're very tolerant of your lifestyle choices.'

'It's not a lifestyle choice,' I shot back. 'I've got extremely dry, and pale, skin.'

Hey, I wasn't lying.

Corina patted me on the back. 'He's very sensitive.'

'You can say that again,' said Amanda.

I kept my hand raised – I really did have a question – but Amanda just rolled her eyes and said, 'It's a figure of speech, Adam. You don't actually need to say it again.'

'Um, Miss Petal,' I asked, ignoring my sister. 'Where are the showers?'

She laughed. And then she laughed again.

'This is the great outdoors,' Petal said. 'We bathe in Mother Nature's bosom.'

'He-he-he.' Nesto giggled. 'That means boobs.'

'He's eleven,' I explained. 'But seriously, I'd like to get cleaned up before we eat.'

53

'We like to keep things natural here,' she explained. 'No showers, no flushing toilets, not even—'

'I'm with Mr Clean* here,' said Corina. 'I don't do outhouses.'

'You kids'll get used to it! And whatever doesn't kill you makes you tastier.'

Huh? Did she just say—

'Stronger,' Petal said, with a sheepish look. 'I must be hungry. Yep, almost dinner time. *Stronger.* I meant stronger.'

---

* Mr Clean was the bald, buff face of a cleaning product. He wasn't so much a superhero as much as he was a god. I kind of loved Corina even more for calling me Mr Clean.

8

In Which I Eat a Feast

They say that the way to a man's heart is through his stomach. While I think that phrase shows a gross misunderstanding of basic anatomy, there is something about good food that makes everything else seem bearable.*

Whatever doubts I had – and they were many, and outlined in a strongly worded letter to my parents – quickly faded to minor annoyances when we entered the dining cabin they called the 'mess hall'.

I must admit my expectations were low. Any place called a mess hall was bound to be messy, and I feared the food would be crueller than gruel. But as we entered

---

* You know, I actually have no idea who 'they' are, but I'm pretty sure (and my mom's a doctor, okay) that you cannot get to anyone's heart through their stomach. Intestines, yes, but heart, I don't think so.

the large log cabin propped up just above the ground on concrete struts, we joined about a hundred other campers at long wooden tables and benches, already laid out with juice, bread baskets, and bizarrely, bowls of candy.

'I'm in heaven,' said Nesto.

'Not yet.' Growl laughed, suddenly behind us and putting his hands on our shoulders. 'Wait 'til you taste it! And you get to eat like this for two whole weeks!'

An overflowing buffet ran the length of one wall. I noticed piping hot pizza, roast chicken, a roast beef carvery, a French-fry station and a freezer counter filled with at least twenty different ice-cream flavours.

It had been a long bus ride and despite the doughnut break, I was famished. I was ready for a feast.

'I actually can't wait,' I said, salivating over the spread.*

'You can eat as much as you like here,' Growl said.

Nesto actually jumped up and down. 'Keeps. Getting. Better!'

'I don't see anything vegan,' complained Corina.

---

* Note: I did not actually salivate on the food as my sister was prone to do when she wanted to claim something for herself, like a cookie or piece of cake. She'd literally lick the food, her germs festering on the top of the cookie and thus warding everyone else off.

'Don't worry,' said Growl. 'We cater for all tastes here. We don't want you to be hungry, so I'll check with the chef.'

Petal pointed to the trays and cutlery. 'As the new arrivals, you campers get to eat first.'

The new campers cheered.

'I love this place,' said Nesto. 'So much food!'

'I hate this place,' countered Corina. 'Too much good cheer.'

For me, I wasn't sure what to think. The food looked amazing, but something felt strange. I grabbed a tray and wiped it down with a fresh wet wipe straight from the packet.

Never leave home without 'em.

Seriously, never.

Ever.

Ever.

I couldn't believe it, but I was actually missing Mom and Dad. I wondered how they were faring on their road trip. Turned out I'd been right about the Founding Fathers, but Amanda had reneged on our bet. But the joke was on her. Even though we weren't in the wilds of Montana, she couldn't get any mobile coverage up here in the sticks of Ontario.

While I certainly didn't wish to be squished in the back seat of a Meltzer family road trip, I did miss Mom and Dad. So, in honour of my money-grubbing parents, I opted for the pizza and scanned the buffet for meatballs.

'Something missing from the spread?' The guy behind the counter must've noticed my glancing. He was skinny, pale, and wearing a hairnet, which I totally approved of, and his arms were inked with circular tattoos. His name tag branded him as Crow.

'I was hoping for meatballs, Mr Crow,' I said.

'With pizza?' he asked. 'What a great pairing. Oh, and it's not Mister.'

'Oh, sorry,' I said. '*Señor* Crow.'

'Just Crow,' he said. 'Meatballs with pizza, pretty great.'

'Actually on the pizza,' I clarified. 'It's my dad's recipe.'

'Homesick, eh?' Crow asked, serving me a couple of slices.

'Maybe a little bit,' I said. 'Okay, a lot.'

'Well, I'll be sure to have meatballs for ya tomorrow. Until then, you ever try poo-teen?'

I stared blankly. 'Poo what?'

'Poutine, pee-oh-you-tee-eye-en-ee,' he said, in a type

of French accent that reminded me of Professor Plante, the mad scientist who tried to unleash a swarm of zombees on Croxton. Even though I missed my parents, I was actually happy to be far from my weird town, which on a normal day was an epicentre of weirdness, but right now, with a convention of thousands of vampires taking over, was at least vamp-point-eight on the Richter scale.

Crow scooped up a plate of fries and doused them with steaming gravy. My mom had a thing for gravy fries, but Crow took it one step further. He suddenly covered them in something called cheese curds.[*] 'It's a big thing up here. I think you'll like it.'

I wasn't sure whether to drool or retch.

I enjoyed a good French fry, a staple of the American diet, and I'd snuck a few of my mom's gravy fries from time to time, so I was no purist, but the addition of cheese (and cheese curds at that!) was either genius or sadistic. Either way, I was certain the plate of gravy-and-cheese-slathered fries would push me way over the

[*] From what I remember from nursery rhymes, Little Miss Muffet liked to eat them with whey. She also sat on a tuffet which I can only assume is an old-fashioned word for her tush.

suggested calorie intake of a boy my age. I might be the walking dead, but I did not need to be the rolling dead.

'Go on,' said Crow, 'you only live once!'

If I was out in the open about being a zombie, I would have debated this, but I wasn't, and he continued, 'Trust me. You'll love 'em!'

So I took my pizza and my poutine (which had nothing to do with either poo or being a teen) and added a generous helping of salad on the side plus a glass of milk, and found my friends at our table.

Corina pushed a few peas around her plate while Nesto had three plates all heaving with meat. A lot of animals died for his dinner.

'Looks like you're a hungry hippo,' said Corina, eyeing my tray.

'I'm trying the local delicacy,' I said, spearing a soggy fry and cheese curd with my fork. As I popped it into my mouth, the grease and salt awoke my taste buds to this northern sensation. 'Oh Canada! It's really good,' I said with my mouth full.

'You boys just don't have self-restraint,' she said, popping a pea into the air and catching it in her mouth.

Corina opened her black leather jacket and teased a plastic bag of Pop Rocks out of her inside pocket.

'Self-restraint's for losers,' said Nesto.

'And for people who wear seat belts,' I added. 'They tend to be winners in Darwin's eyes.'*

I inhaled most of my sopping fries and saved a few at the end for an experiment with my pizza. I laid six gravy soaked fries and three cheese curds on top of the pepperoni slice. At first I felt bad that I was cheating on Dad's meatball pizza. But then I didn't care. It all tasted so good. As I gulped my glass of milk, Petal glided between the tables and stopped behind us. She was carrying a tray with different-coloured squeezy bottles: brown, pink, red, yellow, even green.

'That milk is missing something,' Petal said.

'Yeah,' said Corina. 'The baby cow it was intended for.'

She gave a half laugh and raised the brown squeezy bottle, offering me 'a splash of chocolate?'

Dark brown syrup slipped out of the nozzle and turned my white milk into a cloudy, then chocolaty treat.

Nesto held out his glass, excitedly. 'I'll take them all!'

* Charles Darwin is the guy who put forth the idea of evolution, which means he wouldn't be welcome in most of Ohio's churches. But I think he's amazing.

Petal turned Nesto's milk black with her colourful cocktail of syrup. 'And you?' she asked Corina.

'I'm vegan,' Corina announced.

'I'm so sorry,' the LIT said, suddenly a lot less bubbly. 'Well, I suppose there's always one.'

At that, she rushed away, down the long table and stopped at another group of campers, dousing their milks with sugary syrup and making them really happy campers.

'I never want to leave,' declared Nesto.

Corina rolled her eyes and popped a Rock. She seemed distant, aloof. I mean, those were her normal characteristics, but since this whole camp thing came up she seemed even more detached.

Nesto stuffed his face and I polished off my plate in record time. I was hungrier than I thought and happy to know that my zombified digestive system was still ticking. I had no idea if the food I was eating these days would help me to grow, or whether I'd be stuck in a twelve-year-old's decomposing body for the rest of my life. But what I really felt was full. And it felt really good.

I leaned back in my chair to give my stomach a bit of extra room and relished the sensation of feeling stuffed.

'Just look at them all,' said Corina, gesturing to the mess hall full of carnivorous campers. 'They're gobbling everything in sight.'

She looked at us both. 'And you two are no better.'

'What's wrong?' I asked.

'What's wrong is that you are all going to get really fat.'

'Oh,' I said, 'and downing nothing but Pop Rocks is the diet of champions?'

Corina leaned in. 'I've got a vampire's metabolism,' she whispered.

'Well, there'll be more of us to love,' joked Nesto.

'No, lizard brain,' she said, rising to leave. 'There'll be more of you to eat!'

She kept her mouth closed. I'm pretty sure it wasn't because she had nothing else to say but because her fangs were fighting to come out.

Corina had a bad case of the munchies and I worried that Pop Rocks weren't going to cut it.

9

In Which Corina Tastes Blood

After dinner, the LITs filed us out into the fields and brought us down to the outdoor theatre for the big talent show.

'It's a Nowanakidda tradition,' cheered Growl. 'The campers on their last night put on a show for the newcomers. That's you!'

The theatre was more like a large hole dug out of the gravel, with a semicircle of tiered 'seating' looking down on a flat gravelled stage area.

'Can I get a cushion?' I asked.

Growl laughed. 'Hey Adam, this is open-air theatre, Greek style.'

'Like the yogurt?' asked Nesto. 'So creamy, so tasty.'

I'd seen pictures of Greek amphitheatres filled with toga-wearing ancients watching a play about men gouging their eyes out while what they called a Greek chorus* looked on (not helping).

'Nesto, you can't possibly be hungry?' snarked Corina. 'Ever.'

Growl crouched down to our level. 'Hey, if it's good enough for the ancient Greeks, it's gotta be good enough for us.'

'It didn't exactly end well for them, did it?'

'You're not really a normal twelve-year-old, are you Adam?'

I shook my head. 'Nope.'

'And Ernesto, if you're still hungry, we've got s'mores later.'

'S'more of what?' he asked.

'Exactly!' Growl replied. 'Ah, here comes tonight's entertainment.'

Fifteen campers bounded onto the stage and took a bow. They were tanned, enthusiastic, and full of energy. But something else struck me. They all looked a little, well . . . well fed.

I spotted Corina inhale and then bite her lip.

'You okay?' I asked, quietly.

* Mental note: don't go to Greece.

65

She shook her head, now licking her lips. 'Now *I'm* hungry.'

'You can't get by on Pop Rocks alone,' I said, sounding a bit too much like Doctor Mom, urging me to eat up at dinnertime.

'I can't take it,' she said, looking down at her patent leather. 'I need to feed.' Suddenly she looked up, eyeing the kids on stage they way I sized up the buffet . . . just there for the taking.

Onstage, a girl with a chubby face and wild, curly red hair stepped forward and introduced herself as Sarah.

'This may be our last night here,' Sarah said, 'but we're going out with a bang.'

And suddenly, BANG, a puff of smoke erupted onstage and the players filed behind the wooden boards. It was a bit lame as special effects go, but in this hinterland, I had to applaud their effort.

'How long have they been at camp?' I asked Growl.

'Two weeks.'

'And were they always so substantial?' asked Corina.

'Huh?' grunted Growl.

'I think she means pleasantly plump,' I clarified.

'Well that's not very nice,' said Growl.

'She's not a very nice person,' Nesto and I replied in unison.

'They're my Greek chorus,' Corina said. 'And they're right.'

Two of the campers, a boy and a girl, emerged from behind the set decoration and started juggling. As they threw balls and then bowling pins into the air, it was hard to avoid noticing their extra layers bouncing up and down on their tweenage frames.

'See what I mean?' said Corina. It wasn't really a question.

Suddenly, I heard a buzz pass by my ear, and I wondered if Adamini had somehow followed us here. But it was just a mosquito.

'They're healthy kids,' said Growl with a faux-relaxed manner. 'They're having fun, eating well. Camp is the best time of their lives, and maybe yeah, they put on a little weight up here, but then there's just more of them to—'

Snap!

With lightning-like reflexes, Corina reached out and pinched the buzzing mosquito out of the evening air.

'You're quick,' said Growl. 'Maybe you can use that as your talent when it's your turn.' He turned around to watch a group of outgoing campers start a poorly choreographed medley.

I looked at Corina still holding the squirming mosquito between her finger and thumb.

'It just bit someone,' she said. 'Its body is full of human blood. I can almost taste it.'

'Please don't,' I said. But it was too late. She placed the insect on her tongue and closed her eyes, letting out a satisfied groan.

Nesto watched with both horror and envy. 'Okay, you two can never, ever, ever again say I'm gross because that was—'

'So good,' Corina grunted in a low voice.

'Disturbing,' I said. And I meant it. I didn't know the limits of Corina's self-control, but we were in a fenced-off camp, protected from bears, and these unsuspecting campers were trapped inside with one hungry vampire.

10

In Which the Campers Take a Bow

After the show, which consisted of 'talents' ranging from juggling to gymnastics, the departing campers took their final bow. We applauded politely as one of the camp counsellors, an older girl called Lana, led them offstage and into the darkness of the woods.

Apparently it was camp tradition that the graduating campers put on their final show and then loaded straight onto the bus to drive through the night to return to their normal lives somewhere south of the wilderness.

As they trotted off the stage, Lana led them in a rendition of the Camp Nowannakidda chant like the Pied Piper and they disappeared into the darkness. Corina looked downtrodden and disappointed. Like her dinner had just walked off.

Growl stood up and clapped his hands. He addressed

the hundred or so new campers. There were thirty-four from Croxton, and the other kids, as far as I could tell, came from all over the States. 'That'll be you in two weeks, but right now, it's s'mores by the campfire. C'mon!'

The new crop of campers rose from their hard seats and followed Growl down around the stage and towards the shoreline, where a bonfire was already roaring.

'I'm going to skip the s'mores,' said Corina.

'Yeah,' I said. 'I'm not sure I could do with any more forced fun.'

'Are you kidding, guys?' asked Nesto. 'Marshmallow plus graham cracker plus chocolate equals awe-some-ness.'

'I suggest you go easy on the snacks,' Corina said, patting Nesto's belly. 'Unless you want to become a *plump*acabra.'

'Ha!' He laughed. 'I burn, like, a billion calories in chupa mode. I literally can't eat enough. I'll have so much energy I can chup it up every night!'

'I'm going to hit the coffin,' Corina said. 'Try to sleep off this hunger. You boys enjoy your overeating.'

Corina disappeared into the woods and Nesto urged me down to the shoreline.

'Nesto,' I called, 'wait up. I'm worried about Corina.'

'You're always worried, Adam. This is camp, you know – fun time. I think this is where you should relax and, well – don't take this the wrong way – stop being *you*.'

'Maybe, but I don't want Corina to stop being her. And I don't think she should be alone right now.'

'You think she might eat those happy campers before they go?' he asked, pretty much reading my mind.

'I don't know,' I said. 'But I think friends don't let friends eat people.'

'When you put it *that* way . . .' said Nesto. 'I'll skip the s'mores and come with you.'

We darted into the woods, leaving the newbie campers behind, and followed the graduating campers through the forest. They weren't hard to follow because they'd started singing the Camp Nowannakidda camp song.

We tracked them to the open fields beyond the dining hall, but couldn't spot Corina.

The waiting school bus was purring like a kitten suffering from hay fever. The campers joyously jumped onto their yellow chariot. I pushed a little closer, while hiding in the bushes. I tried to spot anything weird, but realised that the only weird thing was *us*: a zombie in make-up sneaking around in the woods with a bottled-up chupacabra.

Lana ticked their names off a list as each camper boarded the bus. She smiled and gave the occasional hug or high five.

'See you next summer!' one of the campers cheered.

'I'll be here,' she replied with a smile.

As the last of the kids boarded the bus, I finally realized what I didn't see: *their luggage*.

These campers were shipping out to head back to their homes and yet they had no duffel bags, no wheelies, not even a backpack. I wondered, *where was all their stuff?*

And, where were they really going?

The school bus rumbled forth and disappeared through the fence's gates.

'That's them off,' said Lana. 'You got all their bags, Dukie?'

The really tanned camp counsellor in a sleeveless T-shirt and ripped jeans, stepped out of the darkness. 'Got 'em all sorted.'

'Thanks Dukie,' said Lana. 'You're the best.'

'I know it, my fans know it, and now you know it,' he said with a laugh.

'So long as we meet quota,' she said. 'We've got a big summer.'

'It's all good,' replied Duke. 'You gotta relaxi in the taxi.'

'Guess so,' said Lana. 'So long as she has enough campers, it won't be us on the bus.'

Suddenly, I felt a tap on my shoulder – like a drop of dry ice.

I turned around to see Corina's pale face in the moonlight.

'Something weird is going on,' I said.

'Yeah,' she said. 'You boys are following me.'

'Adam was worried,' said Nesto.

'That's nothing new,' said Corina.

'What was that?' Lana said from the woods beyond the clearing.

I shushed Nesto and Corina with the most aggressive finger-on-lips mime I could muster.

Duke shone his flashlight all around. We ducked down to avoid the beam. 'Probably just an animal.'

'Yeah, probably,' Lana agreed. 'There's a herd of moose that's been hanging around the perimeter, and last week Growl spotted a bear.'

'Too bad we can't add them in,' Duke said with a laugh.

'You know the rules,' said Lana. 'Say, you coming for s'mores?'

'I think I've earned it,' he said, as they disappeared into the darkness.

I had no idea what they were talking about but as soon as they were gone, Corina skulked off. Nesto and I followed her into the woods.

'Hey,' I whispered. 'Are you okay?'

She stopped and turned. 'I don't appreciate being spied on.'

'Corina,' I said. 'We weren't spying, we were looking for you. I was worried.'

'I'm fine,' she said with a huff.

'You're not fine,' I said.

'Adam thought you were going to go all-you-can-eat on that busload of kids.'

I looked at Nesto and tilted my head accusingly. 'Way to throw me *under* the bus.'

'You think that little of me, Adam?' asked Corina. 'Listen, Adam, I appreciate your concern, but I just needed some time alone, not to be stalked.'

'I stalk because I care,' I said.

'Yeah, I care too,' said Nesto, then turned back to me to whisper, 'What are we caring so much about?'

'You boys have fun,' said Corina. 'I'm going to bed, for real.'

With that, she took the path back towards the tents and faded from sight, leaving Nesto and me under the starry sky.

'Go on,' I said. 'Go get your s'mores.'

'Really?' he asked excitedly.

I nodded, claiming, 'I'll be along in a few minutes.' Something else was troubling me even more than a moody, hungry vampire. Something just didn't seem right with Camp Nowannakidda and I wanted to find out more.

11

In Which I Find Too Many Shoes

I sneaked back into the clearing where the campers had loaded onto the bus. It was covered in gravel and each footstep made a scratchy sound. I stepped as softly as I could. I wasn't doing anything wrong, except for not joining in the campfire, but I still didn't want to get caught.

At the far left of the clearing, I spotted a barn that I hadn't noticed before. It was painted dark red and from up close blocked out the stars. I didn't hear any animals mooing or clucking inside, so I decided to take a peek.

The barn door was huge and looked like it could fit the whole bus inside. As quietly as I could I lifted the heavy steel latch and slid the door aside. It was pitch-dark inside, but a musty smell hit me like I was in a second-hand clothes shop.

I had recently become a customer of those places

when I was forced to buy back some of my favourite clothes. My mom had donated all of my clothes when she (wrongly, though understandably) assumed I wasn't coming back from the dead. But when I did, I bought back my favourite pair of no-iron jeans, an off-white button-down shirt, and my limited edition NinjaMan necktie (for special occasions, like should I ever get invited to a NinjaMan movie premiere), but I couldn't find my collection of MetaWars socks. Seriously, who buys second-hand socks?

I couldn't see anything in the dark but curiosity compelled me to see what was inside. I fumbled for a light switch and finally, three overhead bulbs clicked on, revealing piles of clothes, shoes, and yes, even socks. My nose had been right, it was like a goodwill shop without the clothes racks or elevator music.

I stood there, frozen and confused. I didn't understand why hundreds, thousands probably, of kids' shirts, shorts, shoes, and socks were piled up in some creepy barn. I wondered, *Where were their owners?*

I suddenly felt very afraid and very alone.

'Doing some late-night shopping?' called a girl's voice behind me.

It turned out I wasn't alone.

'Or snooping?' she added.

I turned to see Lana, the camp counsellor who had loaded the senior campers onto their magical-mystery bus, silhouetted in the square doorway.

'You startled me,' I said, suddenly afraid.

'And you surprised me,' she said.

'I, um, wanted to wave off the campers,' I lied. 'You know, give them one final standing ovation for their amazing talent show.'

'That'll be you in two weeks,' she said. 'I'm Lana.'

'Oh, I'm Adam, Adam Meltzer. This is my first day at camp.'

'Then you haven't heard about our ... clothing charity,' she said. I couldn't tell if she was asking me or telling me.

I just shook my head.

'At the end of every session, we ask the campers to donate as many of their clothes as they can spare to help the needy. At the end of summer, the camp makes sure the clothes and shoes and stuff—'

'Socks too?'

'We'll take it all. We make sure it all gets washed and given to charities then handed out to the less fortunate at Christmastime.'

'Oh,' I said, suddenly feeling a bit foolish for feeling so ghoulish. 'That's a relief.'

'What do you mean?' she asked.

I somehow didn't feel right revealing my morbid anxiety about the piles of clothes, so I tap-danced a bit.* 'You know, that you guys actually wash the clothes first. On a high heat, with antibacterial soap and fabric softener.'

'Sounds like doing laundry is your talent, Adam,' she said with a smile, leading me out and closing up the barn door.

'It's just a hobby,' I said.

'Talent show's in just two weeks,' she said. 'What *is* your talent?'

I was about to say, 'rising from the grave', but I certainly didn't want to reveal my undead status. 'Dancing,' I said. 'I'm a pretty good dancer.'

I was doing myself down. I'm not just pretty good, I'm zomtastic. Since returning from the dead, I'd kept practising at Sunshine Studios, and I actually think my rhythm and timing had improved in my afterlife.

---

* It's just an expression. I didn't actually tap dance. First, I wasn't wearing the right shoes, and second, the gravel ground would have torn the metal taps to shreds.

We walked back through the woods and then across the fields. Lana told me her life story. She was born in somewhere called Sarnia, Ontario and always wanted to go to camp when she was my age.

'In my last year of high school, I was working at a doughnut shop when this camp advertised for counsellors. So I signed up and made the cut. I'm in university now, studying to be a teacher, probably for kids your age, actually, but coming up here in the woods is like a dream job.'

My suspicions started to fade. She was pretty normal, and not at all weird as I'd expected. 'Can I ask you a question, Lana?' I asked.

'Anything, Adam.'

'Why does everyone up here like doughnuts so much?'

She laughed. 'Ha, yeah, we do . . . we're Canadian. It's in the blood I guess.'

In the blood.

It made me think of Corina, and what a tough time she was having. She was hungering for human blood and although she projected an iron will, I couldn't be sure that at some point she wouldn't snap and go on a bloodsucking rampage, especially up here in the woods . . . with no phone signal and no witnesses. It felt like the perfect place for a vampire massacre. She chose to be a vegan, but being a vampire was ... *in the blood.*

'Can I ask *you* a question?' Lana asked.

'Anything,' I said. I mean, she could ask anything she wanted, but that didn't mean I had to answer.

'What were you really doing snooping around?' she asked. 'I won't tell anyone, I'm just curious.'

'Well,' I said, buying some time for my thankfully still-firing neurons to work out the best response. 'If this isn't too forward, do things seem a little *strange* to you here?'

'What do you mean by *strange?*'

'Um, are you guys deliberately fattening up us campers?'

'Deliberately?' She laughed. 'We can't keep you little guys away from the grub!'

'It just seems—'

'Adam, enjoy it. This camp is supposed to be an escape for you guys, away from school, away from your families, away from dinner-time rules that say you can't have ice cream before your main meal. This is a place to let loose and have fun, and if this isn't too forward, you strike me as the kind of guy who has trouble letting go and having fun.'

81

'I have fun,' I said. 'In my own way. Ideally with indoor plumbing.'

As we approached the campfire area, the flames were dying but the singing wasn't. The happy campers were singing about a camel called Alice.

Alice the camel had five humps.

'I would've given anything at your age to go to camp, so enjoy it. For me, for that girl who never had the chance. Now get in there.'

Alice the camel had four humps.

'Okay,' I agreed, exhaling and sitting down on a log beside Ernesto and Corina. Corina looked bored, and Nesto's face was covered in marshmallow and chocolate.

Alice the camel had three humps.

'What's with the escort?' asked Corina.

'Thought you were going to bed?' I said.

'Thought I'd try to control the hunger,' she said, 'instead of hiding from it. Speaking of hiding?'

'I got a little lost,' I said, not fully fessing up to my secret snooping.

Alice the camel had two humps.

'Hey, Corina,' I said. 'I'm sorry about following you like that. I just wanted to make sure you were all right.'

Alice the camel had one hump.

'It's cool,' she said. 'I'm glad you're back. I was starting to get a little, well, worried.'

'Worried? You?' I teased.

'I know. That's your department.'

'Well, I think you were right. I should just give the worrying a break, at least for these two weeks.'

Alice the camel had no humps.

'Cos Alice was a horse!' Ernesto shouted. I looked at him, filthy face, clapping madly, and decided to let go and have some fun.

What was the worst that could happen?

12

In Which I Am Awoken by a Moose (Story)

I was settled in for a summer slumber, dreaming of a washing machine big enough to wash all the newly donated clothes I'd found, when I felt a cool breeze blow over me. At first I thought I was in the spin cycle, but it was just my tentmate waking me up.

'Adam, are you awake?' Nesto said, climbing back into the tent.

'I am now,' I said. 'Where were you?'

'It's a long story,' Nesto said.

I closed my eyes again, hoping to will myself back to sleep. I really wanted to fill the tray with gallons of detergent.

'But we've got time,' he added.

As Nesto crawled back into his sleeping bag, he told me about his night-time adventure.

'I really needed to pee, and I saw that your water bottle was empty. I thought about just bottling it in here and saving myself the trip—'

'Whoa, Nesto.' I stopped him, looking at my mostly empty water bottle beside me. 'How much time did you spend thinking that?'

'Don't worry, not too long. And a good thing too, because ... I'm in love.'

'What are you talking about?' I asked.

'Okay,' he said, 'so I thought that peeing in your bottle would kind of upset you—'

'You think?'

'That's why I crept out as quietly as I could. But instead of going to the outhouses—'

'Yeah, I've been avoiding those,' I confessed.

'You're gonna burst sooner or later,' Nesto said.

I knew he was right – I couldn't avoid nature calling, even up here in the middle of nature.

'So I marked my territory along the fence line and feeling free, changed into chupa mode. I ran around on all fours feeling ... well, like me. And that's when I heard it. It was like a low, loud bullhorn sound. It came from the trees beyond the fence, and I howled back.

'Then it blew again. It made me think of music lessons at school, but you know, more melodic. It was definitely an animal. Except it wasn't. Through the trees walked a . . . *girl*. A really, really pretty, like magazine cover or Disney Channel, girl.

'I'd totally forgotten I was still in chupa mode and she came up to the fence and waved. Then she let out that sound again, like she had a trombone stuck in her throat.'

I'd worried that I'd nodded off and was actually dreaming. 'Wait a sec, Nest. Did you say you met a girl tonight?'

'Crazy, I know!' he said. 'But it gets crazier. She's not just a girl.'

I got it. 'That's cool, man. I used to have an imaginary friend when I was younger too.'

'Adam, she's real, she's beautiful, and guess what?'

'Um, what?' I asked, still unsure if I was dreaming this.

'She's a moose.'

Now I was confused. 'A real, beautiful . . .'

'Moose. A *were*moose,' he said. 'She lives in the woods with her herd, and just like me, she switches between animal and normal kid.'

'Nesto,' I said, stopping him in his tracks, 'you're not a normal kid.'

'And neither is she. She's awesome! Her name is Melissa. She likes frolicking in the forest, drinking from streams, and, get this, she likes to poo outside too!'

'Sounds like your soulmate.'

'I know, right!' he squealed. 'As if this place could get any better.'

'So are you going to see Melissa the moose again?'

'Oh yeah. After campfire, tonight, when she can sneak away from her herd.'

'That's great, Nesto. I'm really pleased for you.'

'Thanks, Adam. I've never been happier.'

I turned over, not quite sure what to believe, and finally dozed back asleep.

13

In Which I Become a Happy Camper

The thing about sleeping in a tent, besides the fact that you're on the ground, which should be the sole domain of worms and insects, is that *rise and shine* comes early.

Nobody told me to bring an eyemask, so when the sun rose, so did I. Nesto was still snoring beside me when the morning rays acted as a natural, if annoying, alarm clock. I unzipped the tent and stretched my limbs. Slowly, a few of the other newbie campers were rousing and I spotted Amanda, holding her phone like a divining rod.

My sister was famous, at least within the Meltzer extended family, for sleeping through just about anything. So I walked over to see what was up, since she was up.

'What are you doing awake so early?' I asked.

'It's too bright, and I can't get a signal here.'

'I don't think the camp is big on mobile phones,' I said.

'Then it needs to get with the programme. How can I Instagram anything? I mean, how will anyone know what I'm doing?'

I must admit, I did fancy calling Mom and Dad to let them know we'd arrived safely and to check in on their big road trip.

'We could write postcards,' I said.

'Or smoke signals,' she teased.

Suddenly, I heard a rapid zip. 'YOU MELTZERS ARE TOO LOUD.'

It was Corina, crawling out of her and Amanda's tent.

'Hey, roomie!' chirped Amanda. 'Sun get you up too?'

'No, I came prepared for light, but not for noise,' she said, peeling back the tent flap, revealing her all-black sleeping bag that zipped up and over her head . . . like a portable coffin.

'Well, you're up now. Are you hungry?' Corina shot me an are-you-kidding look, and I clarified. 'Ready for breakfast?'

'You know they have fifteen flavours of liquorice here,' said Amanda. 'They have a liquorice bar. It's even open at breakfast!'

'Someone say breakfast?' growled Ernesto, clambering out of our tent on all fours. 'I'm starving.'

'No,' said Corina, 'you're hardly starving after how you stuffed your face yesterday!'

'Did you get dressed in the dark?' Nesto asked. 'Because you've got your grumpy pants on.'

I got dressed (in perfectly normal tracksuit trousers), expertly applied my zombie-concealing make-up, and joined the others on their breakfast pilgrimage.

Despite the absence of the campers that left last night, the dining hall was just as buzzy and the food was piled just as high.

'Hey, my man Adam,' called Crow. 'Your meatball pizza's on the menu tonight!'

'I didn't know they did requests,' said Nesto. 'I'm going to ask for my favourite, squirrel tacos.'

After downing orange juice, three pancakes, two waffles and a flight of bacon strips that were drizzled in honey, I was feeling ready to go outside and face the day.

'Arts and crafts this morning campers,' announced Growl. 'We'll stay in here while you create your masterpieces.'

*

Arts and crafts took on a surprisingly competitive bent when Growl explained that our creations would be judged by the camp's owner.

'This is a chance to show off your creativity,' he said. 'The challenge today is to build the best gingerbread building you can. It could be a house, a monument, anything you want. The bigger, bolder and more creative, the better. And tonight, before dinner, the camp's owner is going to come to inspect you – I mean your creations – and hand out a prize for the best one. And then after dinner, the best part, you can eat them!'

The camp counsellors unveiled trays of baked gingerbread in all shapes and sizes, and buckets of sweets for decorations, and handed each of us a piping bag filled with icing. I'd dabbled in cake decoration on rainy Saturday mornings with Mom, so I felt that I had a built-in advantage.

Nesto, Corina, and I collected our materials and claimed a table to get building.

'What are you guys going to build?' I asked my friends.

'This mess hall, I think,' said Nesto. 'It's my new favourite place in the world.'

'Transylvania Castle,' said Corina, leaning in to whisper. 'It's the one building every vampire knows by heart.'

'How 'bout you, Adam?' nudged Nesto.

I thought of my Broadway dreams and figured if I couldn't bring Adam Meltzer to the Great White Way, I could bring Broadway to me. 'I'm going to build a replica of the Radio City Music Hall in New York City.'

We spent the morning building our masterpieces, and I must admit (and I'm biased here) that my shrine was stunning. Corina's was pretty great too. She'd covered it in dark grey icing and made little skulls out of white marshmallows.

'Of course in real life, those are actual human skulls,' she explained, 'pulled off the spines of the Count's enemies.'

'Of course,' I agreed.

Before I knew it, Growl was calling, 'Time for lunch!'

Instead of keeping us in the dining hall, he led us down to the lakefront where smoke rose from behind the trees. The smell of grilling meat wafted onshore and we discovered that a big BBQ had been set up.

I still felt full from breakfast, but the sizzling hot dogs and burgers smelled too good to pass up.

Corina looked glum, and hungry, until Petal showed her a separate BBQ covered in grilled vegetables.

'You made a special one just for me?' she asked, surprised.

'We want everyone to feel welcome here,' said Petal, 'and be well fed.'

'Hey, can we go swimming this afternoon?' asked Nesto.

I preferred my bodies of water to be highly chlorinated, but the hot midday sun sparkled on the lake, making it look as inviting as untreated water could possibly be.

'Baseball after the BBQ, and then swimming before the judging,' said Growl.

'Um, Growl,' I said. 'Are the sports optional?'

'Adam's not really the physical type,' said Corina.

'I just don't like games with balls. Or bats. Or balls being thrown at bats that then get hit into the air at high speeds. Maybe we could play curling instead? That's a Canadian sport and is kind of like sweeping up vigorously on ice.'

'Curling's a winter sport, Adam. But you're American, and baseball's the great American game, isn't it?'

'Great.' I sighed. I knew I couldn't hit, throw, or field, and it was just a matter of time before I made a complete fool of myself on the diamond. Of course, I had no idea this would be the very least of my worries.

14

In Which I Get Taken Out
of the Ball Game

We were split up into two teams and given pre-worn red and blue vests to wear over our clothes. I raised my hand in protest.

'Do you have anything, um, factory fresh?' I asked.

'You crack me up, Adam,' said Growl.

That really wasn't my intention, but since everybody else had donned their colours, I didn't want to hold up their fun. I slithered into the used red vest, trying not to let it touch my skin. Nesto and I were on the same team, and Corina was blue, along with Jake and my sister.

Fortunately, Growl had a bag of brand-new Camp Nowannakidda baseball caps.

'Pick your positions kids. Reds in the field first and blues at bat,' said Growl.

In baseball, the field is separated into an infield where all the action is, and an outfield where a batter may occasionally hit a ball – and I wasn't looking for action.

'I prefer to be as far away from the ball as possible,' I said.

'Okay, Adam's in the outfield,' said Growl.

'Is there such a thing as out-outfield?' I asked.

'If there's a fly ball, it's all you!'

'Lucky duck,' said Nesto, who volunteered for shortstop, the fielder between second and third base, which I thought was wholly appropriate given his height. 'I love fresh flies.'

I was in left field, furthest from the bench and hopefully furthest from the ball.

Amanda was up first and struck out. We Meltzers, clearly, were not a sporty bunch.

Second up to bat was Corina and she ended up slamming the ball into the sky. It soared over the infield like a comet as it rushed down towards me at terminal velocity. I faintly heard my team cheering me on to catch it, but it was moving too fast. My hand sweated in my glove and I couldn't raise it on time.

Thwop!

The ball dented the grass beside me. I heard a collective groan from the reds as Corina glided around the bases and comfortably hopped onto home plate, doing a little victory dance. She high-fived her teammates as the next batter stepped up to the plate.

When it was our turn at bat, Corina volunteered to pitch. She got two players out by the time I was called to the plate.

I grabbed the bat, very aware that the last time I had swung at anything, it was the robot-shaped piñata on my birth/death day. I still couldn't believe my life had ended that day, now well over four months ago, and then had started anew with a rebirth from the grave.

I was lost in thought when Corina taunted me on my way to the plate. 'Batter up,' she called. 'I'm throwin' cannons.'

I didn't want to embarrass myself like I did in the field, so I reluctantly stepped forward, gripped the bat and prepared to meet Corina's pitch.

Corina swung her leg into the air like they do on TV and unleashed the fury of her immortal power. I swung as hard as I could but, instead of hitting the ball, the ball hit me.

Corina's curve ball pounded me in the head, knocking me down and out. The sunshine quickly faded and all went dark as I blacked out.

*

I was back in my coffin, in my grave. It was dark and hot. And then too hot. The coffin lit up with a red glow: a heating element. The inside of my coffin was like the inside of an oven. I was being cooked. I pounded and thrashed at the wooden box but couldn't get out. Finally, the heat was too much and I passed out – baked in my own coffin.

*

I came to and opened my eyes, which was a mistake. The afternoon sun was strong and I squinted until Corina leaned over me, blocking out the sun – a vampire eclipse.

'How many fingers am I holding up?' she asked.

'None,' I said, noticing her hands were by her sides.

'What's your favourite brand of antibac soap?'

It was a trick question. 'GermOff for efficacy, Flower Shower for aroma.'

She pulled me up. 'You'll be fine, slugger.'

But I wasn't so sure. I couldn't shake the awful feeling of my daymare.

15

In Which I Win A Prize

My head had recovered, but I wasn't sure my pride had.

I wasn't built for baseball. It was nothing like choreographed dance where you could rehearse and rehearse to refine every step until it was perfect. With baseball you just had to wing it and that felt unnatural to me.

After the game (Reds 5, Blues 2), we filed back into the mess hall and stood behind our gingerbread masterpieces. I was pretty proud of my Radio City Music Hall and I thought that at least biscuit-based construction was one activity I was built for.

'Ahoy, campers,' said Growl, calling us to attention. 'We are very honoured to have the owner of the camp, Mrs Lebkuchen, with us today to welcome you all to Camp Nowannakidda.'

He started clapping and an old woman, hunched

over with a cane and wearing a black shawl pulled up over her hair, stepped through the kitchen door.

'My dear, dear children,' she said in a foreign accent I couldn't quite place. 'This camp has been in my family for many years. And we have welcomed thousands and thousands of children, like yourselves, through our gates to have a once in a lifetime experience.'

She spoke slowly and sounded much older than she looked. I wasn't sure she was even human. My first instinct was vampire, and I looked over to Corina and mouthed, 'Your kind?'

She shook her head, as if to say *I'm not like her*. But there was something unreal about Mrs Lebkuchen. If not vampire, maybe she was a zombie? But whilst her skin was certainly old and crinkly, it didn't look decayed.

Her accent was definitely not American. She sounded a bit like the European or Russian villains in the NinjaMan movies, but not Spanish or Latin American, so I ruled out chupacabra.

'I was not so lucky as a young girl,' she continued in slow, stuttering speech. 'I grew up very poor in Bavaria, and we didn't have such things as summer camp. But I believe children should have fun before they—'

'Go back to school in the fall,' added Growl, helping her along.

'And before you do, I should like to meet each of you,' she said, lowering the shawl off her head and laying it on her hunched shoulders. Mrs Lebkuchen had wiry black hair with coils of white running through it.

Growl led her down the opposite line of tables and she stopped and said hello to each eager competitor. As she examined each creation, I tried to see if I had any real competition. I spotted her chatting to Jake, and she seemed to really like the look of his NinjaCave because she reached out and pinched his chubby cheek. 'Just the way I like it,' I heard her say across the room.

His opus was a near-perfect replica of NinjaMan's secret HQ, and while I didn't take Mrs Lebkuchen for a comic-book fan, she certainly had an eye for art.

Finally, she made her way over to our tables.

'You're too skinny and pale,' said the old woman, turning to Corina. 'In my youth, food was scarce and we nearly starved, but here I put out so much food for you children. A feast every night like I never had.'

'I'm a vegan,' Corina said.

'What does that mean?'

'I don't eat anything that comes from an animal.'

Suddenly, Mrs Lebkuchen slapped her cane on the table. The towers of Transylvania trembled but didn't topple. 'But animals are here to be eaten.'

'I don't see it that way,' replied Corina, calmly.

'It is the *only* way!' cried the camp owner. 'Hunger must be sated.'

'Um,' began Growl, 'perhaps we should—'

'I try to control my hunger,' Corina added. 'I try really hard and it isn't easy, believe me, but I think I'm a better . . . *person* because of it.'

The old woman was shaking. 'Better than *me*?'

Growl escorted the incensed old woman to my creation. She took one look at me and her dark eyes widened.

'Another vegan?' she asked.

'Definitely not,' I said. 'I couldn't live without meatballs.'

'Then why so thin? And this colour on your face, it's not natural is it?'

She stared intently at me, looking me up and down the way Mom might pick out a fish at the market.

'So this is Radio City Music Hall,' I said, trying to shift the subject away from my irreversible skin condition. 'I've always wanted to perform there but—'

'So you're a singer?' she asked. 'Sing an old lady a song?'

'NO!' cried Corina and Nesto to my left.

'We've got a Greek chorus thing going on,' I said awkwardly.

'I love the Greek yogurt,' she said. 'In fact, we're making a Greek-yogurt flavoured doughnut in the new batch.'

I was confused and I must've looked it because Growl explained, 'The Lebkuchen family doesn't just own this camp but they also own the Canadian Nibble Donut Corporation.'

'You own Can Nibble?' I asked excitedly. 'I am completely in love with your product.'

Even Corina nodded her head in agreement.

'I wish they were in the States,' I added.

'Someday soon,' she said with wide grin 'We've just about conquered Canada, but I think the world is nearly ready for our recipes, don't you?'

'Most definitely,' I said. 'I was sceptical at first, but I'm a convert and a cheerleader.'

'We're totally taking some home with us,' said Nesto.

The Bavarian-born doughnut queen of Canada moved down the row to inspect Nesto next.

'Small, but solidly built,' she said.

'Thanks, Mrs Leprechaun,' Nesto said, proudly holding up his model of the mess hall. 'I worked really hard on it.'

'Ernesto,' said Growl. 'It's Leb-ku-hen.'

'Oh,' he said. 'Sorry.'

'It's an old name, from the old country. That's why we bought this camp – this forest reminds us of our ancestors' home in the woods of Bavaria.'

'Well, it's really nice to meet you, Mrs Lebkuchen,' said Ernesto, slowly pronouncing the woman's name. 'But, I'm dying to know. Who's won the contest? Who's the best?'

'The what?' she asked.

'The model making,' said Growl, reminding the old lady, clearly suffering from a bit of dementia, of why she was here.

'Oh, yes, that. Well, I've inspected everybody and I think the winner of this group of campers has got to be, hmm . . .' She looked slowly around the room. Each of the campers smiled, hoping to will her into picking them as the winner.

'That boy over there,' she finally said, pointing her cane at Jake.

'Yes!' he exclaimed. 'NinjaMan rules!'

I was disappointed, but gave Jake a congratulatory wave across the room. He really had made something special.

'What is the prize?' I asked.

'The prize,' she said, 'is that we'll name a new doughnut after you.'

I saw Jake beaming with pride. 'My folks are going to freak,' he said. 'I'll be famous. Well, famous in Canada anyway.'

'And soon the world,' Mrs Lebkuchen reminded him.

'Cool,' said Jake.

Lucky duck, I thought.

16

In Which I Learn the Truth

After stuffing our faces at dinner and destroying our gingerbread creations for dessert, the LITs rounded us up and marched us out of the dining cabin and into the woods. I noticed a dastardly mosquito buzzing around Nesto's neck and, acting on instinct, I went in for the kill.

Slap.

'What'd you do that for?' he asked.

I showed him my palm, now decorated with mosquito guts and blood.

Corina inhaled. 'Even chupa blood smells pretty good.'

'I'm going to go wash this off,' I said. 'Hygiene first.'

I peeled off from the group, marching a well-beaten path through the field and headed towards the wooden restroom hut.

'Where you going, camper?' asked Growl from the front.

I crossed my legs and did the universally accepted pee dance and he instantly understood. He gave me an understanding salute and told me to, 'Hurry back. You don't want to miss the Camp Nowannakidda Chant.'

I was certain I did want to miss any such chant – I had vampire-enticing blood on my hand. But when I opened the wooden door to the boys' bathroom, I froze.

This was no bathroom.

It was an outhouse.

On my left were three stalls, with no more than a wooden plank separating me from the cumulative waste of hundreds, if not thousands, of campers who'd pooped before me, lurking down below in a man-made pit of defecation despair.

On my right was what appeared to count as the hand-washing station at Camp Nowannakidda. Three leaky faucets dripping over one long, stainless-steel[*] basin and one cracked bar of soap that had dirt permanently lodged into its crevices. Half of a mirror hung dangerously above the metal sink and I caught a glimpse of myself looking sweaty and decomposed.

I turned the tap on and reached for the filthy soap.

---

[*] Don't be fooled by the branding. It had plenty of stains.

The lather was brown, so I rubbed the sliver of soap, expunging the remnant dirt and getting down to the untouched, white core underneath. Once I was satisfied I'd rid my hand of the mosquito's ill-gotten dinner, I air-dried my hands (who says there's no use for jazz hands outside the theatre?) and emerged from the stinkroom into the open air of the field.

Beyond the treeline, I could see the orange glow of the campfire and the plume of smoke whisping into the evening sky. And then I heard it - the Camp Nowannakidda Chant.

But the singing voices were quickly upstaged by two camp counsellors chatting as they walked past the outhouse. I slipped back inside the *stink*house because I just didn't feel like being social.

'Whaddya think of this batch?' asked a girls' voice, maybe Petal.

'Too scrawny,' replied an older guy, whom I think was Duke. 'I thought there was supposed to be an obesity crisis.'

I waited for them to pass and peered out of the wooden door. Duke and Petal sauntered towards the mess hall and instinct told me to follow them, keeping my distance.

The two camp counsellors disappeared inside and I found an open window and peeked in. The camp crew were chatting, listening to music and cleaning up.

'Think we'll make quota this summer?' asked Lana.

'You know what happens if we don't,' said Crow. 'Don't worry – two weeks of poutine and sundaes and they'll be ready!'

'Not the vegan,' said Petal. 'I don't know what we're going to do about her. Granny won't be pleased.'

'I'm more worried about that kid in make-up,' said Duke. 'He looks sickly.'

'At least their little friend is eating for the three of them.' Lana laughed.

'Don't worry, guys,' said Petal. 'Growl's a master at this. We'll make quota. I'm sure of it!'

I shifted my weight – my quads were killing me – and fell over.

'What was that?'

'Go check!'

I heard the rapid rush of footsteps on the floorboards and then quickly descending the wooden steps. I looked out to the field but knew I couldn't make the treeline in time.

The only hiding place was under the cabin. I

imagined the space between the ground and cabin's floor was the domain of filthy foxes or rabid field mice. But if I didn't want to get caught snooping around, I really didn't have a choice. I crouched down and prepared to burrow like a badger.

I swung my body under the cabin, quickly entangling myself in a myriad of cobwebs, then felt something squish under my shoulder that I'm pretty sure was fresh animal poo, and continued my roll until I was covered in nature and well and truly hidden from the LITs rushing around the cabin, searching for the source of the alarming noise.

'There's nobody here!' one of them called.

'Probably just an animal,' said another.

'Too bad we can't add 'em to the batch,' joked Lana.

'Humans only, and kids at that,' said Petal. 'You know Mrs Lebkuchen's rules. The Can Nibble Donut Corporation is very particular on its ingredients.'

Can Nibble.

As in . . .

Cannibal.

Oh no, they were going to turn us into doughnuts.

17

In Which I Plot Our Escape

Once our camp counsellor captors had retreated back inside, I scrambled out from under the mess hall, covered in cobwebs and stains that shall forever, well, stain my memory. I ran as fast as two decrepit legs could carry me. It was dark now and I only had the glow of the lakeside campfire to guide me.

I'd eaten a Can Nibble doughnut, and so I'd unknowingly eaten people. I'd become a cannibal. But worse, I'd become a cliché. I'd become the very thing that everyone expected from a zombie: a people eater.

As I raced under the night sky, I worried that maybe this was the start of my descent into rampaging cannibalism. Maybe all of the stereotypes about zombies were true and I was just late to the party?

Maybe deep down, Corina and I were the same. On the surface, we maintained a façade of civility, but underneath we were monsters. Maybe we *all* were.

This camp was clearly up to something evil, but what about all of us who'd tucked into the produce of that evil ... the doughnuts? I wondered if the Canadians, who seemed so nice, knew they were eating children with every nibble of their favourite Nibblers. My head was spinning as I ran, and I wanted to unknow what I now knew.

I suddenly felt very alone. I missed my parents – I really wanted to call them but I couldn't. We had no phones and no contact with the outside world until we broke free of the camp's confines.

As I ran in the darkness, I worried about Corina too. I feared the hunger for humans would soon overcome her. She'd sucked blood and craved more.

I hoped I was different.

I'd accidentally ingested people and was repulsed by the prospect of eating anyone else (sugar-coating or not).

I couldn't stand by while Camp Nowannakidda turned campers into doughnuts. Somehow I had to stop the murderous conspiracy. But first, I needed to get out.

I burst through the treeline and navigated a winding

path to find the campers in a big circle around a bonfire. They took turns holding sticks to the flames, melting marshmallows and chanting camp songs.

> *That's where I want to go.*
> *Back to my Ohio.*
> *Oh I how I long to go . . .*
> *Ho-oh-ohm.*

I spotted Corina in the crowd, not chanting. She sat on a large log with her arms crossed, looking bored. I sat down beside her.

'So we've got a big problem,' I whispered urgently.

'Yeah, way too much camp cheer,' she replied. 'I can't take this much enthusiasm.'

'Where's Ernesto?' I wondered.

'Doing an imitation of a chipmunk,' she said, pointing over towards the raging fire.

Nesto popped a few burnt marshmallows into his cheeks, puffing them out like the breed of rodent that everyone seems to think is adorable.

'Chipmunks,' I vented to no one in particular, 'just rats with stripes.'

'He's stuffing his face while I'm . . . Adam,' she leaned

in to whisper, 'I'm hungry. There's so much life, so much tasty, juicy blood, and it's right here.'

'You gotta fight the urge, Corina,' I said, having no idea how hard that might be. I like to think that I'm a bastion of self-control, but deep down I know I give into my neurotic urges all the time. Who was I to lecture Corina to do any different? 'Because somebody else wants to gorge on these kids too.'

'There's another vampire here?'

'No,' I said, 'this camp isn't a camp at all. It's a farm. A fat farm, getting us plump and ready to be turned into doughnuts.'

'The fumes of the outhouse go to your head?'

They did, yes, and if I ever made it out of Nowannakidda alive (well, *intact*) I'd explore a nose-hair transplant because particles of campers' poo were probably trapped amid my nasal follicles, but that'd have to wait.

'I'm serious,' I said. 'I overheard the camp counsellors. We're all supposed to be ingredients for the Can Nibble Donuts. Can Nibble ... as in *Cannibal*.'

'So *that's* why those donuts taste so good,' she said. 'It isn't the sugar, it's the protein!'

Ernesto bounded back from the fire, his face full of

sugary goop, and mumbled, 'Hi Adam, did you have a good poo?'

'I was just going to wash my hands!' I said in my defence.

'Sure, sure,' he said, gulping down the marshmallows. 'Isn't this great?'

'No, Ernesto. It's all terrible. We've got to get out of here, get everyone out of here, before it's too late.'

'You're such a downer tonight, Adam,' Nesto said. 'I'm having the time of my life. No parents, great food and plenty of room to let my chupa run loose. And . . . I'm in love.'

'Listen Hansel and Gretel,' I said. 'Unless you want to be turned into doughnuts for these cannibalistic Canadians to munch on, we've got to bust out of here. Pronto!'

Nesto tilted his head, looking very confused.

Corina filled him in. 'This camp is fattening us so that we can be eaten.'

'Well that's just rude,' Nesto said.

Corina looked around at the happy campers and asked solemnly, 'How are we going to get everyone out?'

'I have no idea,' I confessed. 'But we have to try.'

18

In Which We Take to the Sea (Well, the Lake)

After the campfire, the leaders shuffled us off to our tents. I looked at each of them with suspicion but did my best not to make my scorn obvious. I didn't want to arouse any unwanted attention.

Nesto snuck off for his moose meetup, which I told him would have to be a goodbye, and I found myself alone in the tent, thinking and worrying:

How were we going to escape?

What insects were in here with me?

How could an entire country become cannibals?

And even if we did escape the camp's perimeter, where would we go?

I heard a scratching on the tent. *Oh great*, I thought, *the weremoose has come calling.*

But it wasn't an animal. It was a vampire. 'Zom-boy, you still up?'

I crept out of my sleeping bag, unzipped the tent and crawled out into the starlit field.

'Nice ninjamas,' she said.

'Thanks,' I said. 'They're from the upcoming movie, not the comic book, but I think they capture the essence of—'

'You don't know when I'm kidding, do you?'

Maybe I didn't, but at least I was wearing one of a limited edition of only one thousand pairs of NinjaMan: The Movie pyjamas and Corina was stuck in her traditional black vampire nightgown.

'At least I'm not dressed for Prom of the Dead,' I said.

'Touché,' she said. 'This is my great-great-grandmother's coffin gown and mother made me promise to wear it at camp.'

Suddenly, Corina threw her arms around me. But I knew better than to expect a hug or other display of affection. She gripped me tight and rose up into the air.

Her coffin gown flowed in the breeze of the night sky and, looking down, I spotted the rows of tents assembled near the treeline. I took in the lay of the land. The campfire area was down to the right, nestled against the eastern shore of the lake. The mess hall was inland, near the baseball diamond, and I followed my finger to trace where the barn would be in the woods to the north. Behind the barn was another clearing where half a dozen cabins sat. I supposed that was where the counsellors slept. The camp was penned in on three sides by the razor-wire fence, and to the west by the lake's shore. There was only one gated road in and out. Since we couldn't guarantee that everyone could swim across, and I didn't think we could risk outing Corina as a flying vampire, we'd have to flee under the fence.

Corina flew us over to the top of a pine tree and I sat myself on a branch.

'Let's try not to kill any drug dealers this time,' I said.*

She laughed. 'So what's your plan, Stan?'

'Who's Stan?' I wondered. 'Is he a camper? Someone you're interested in?'

'Forget about it,' she said. 'Listen, I just wanted to say sorry for being so grumpy. I meant what I said to

---

* The last time I was up in a tree with Corina, she pushed me off and I crushed the town drug dealer. Corina turned him into a vampire to stop him from being my murder victim. She was that kind of friend.

that old witch Mrs Lebkuchen – it's really hard keeping the hunger at bay. At least up here I can't smell the campers' blood. It's not so bad.'

But there was something I could smell. Something familiar, something delicious.

I took a big sniff and smelled doughnuts – freshly made. Somewhere on the dark horizon a doughnut factory was turning plumped-up campers into tasty treats.

'We have to get out of here, tonight,' I said. 'Get help, call the authorities and then get everyone to safety.'

'Maybe he can dig us out,' she said, spotting Ernesto down below at the fence.

Just then I heard a bullhorn sound. A moose call. 'If we can pull him away from his chupa-crush,' I joked.

Corina put her arms around me and we floated down towards the treeline. She hovered us along the edge of the field, about twenty feet up in the air. A howling hiss filled the air – Ernesto's love call. I pointed to the bush below.

'Down there,' I said.

We landed softly on a floor of pine needles and found chupa Nesto on his hind claws, rubbing noses through the chain-link fence with an enormous moose.

Corina cleared her throat. 'Well, isn't this sweet?'

'Is that her?' I asked.

The moose turned to me and in a perfectly normal, though I would say slightly snarky, voice said, 'Of course it's *her*. And yes, it *is* sweet. Nesty's said a lot of nice things about you two, but never mentioned you were both masters of the completely obvious.'

Corina and I looked at each other. That moose really put us in our place.

Nesto turned around and shrugged. 'We are kind of having a moment here guys, do you mind?'

'Nesto,' I interrupted. 'Can you dig us out of this camp? There's a fence all around the perimeter ... we're trapped!'

'Is he always so demanding?' demanded the moose.

'More like needy,' said Nesto. 'And he wants to escape from camp.'

'Homesick, eh?' asked Melissa.

'I'm not needy and I'm not homesick,' I said. 'But we need to get out of Camp Cannibal before it's too late. Ernesto, please, can you dig us out?'

Melissa the moose pressed her head into the chain-link fence. It rattled all the way along into the darkness. 'Do you think Nesty and I'd be playing nosey-nose at the fence if he could?'

'Good point,' I said. This moose had a lot of sass, but she also talked a lot of sense.

Nesto clawed at the ground. 'It's all concrete under there,' he said. 'And the top of the fence is electric. Believe me, I tried.'

'Then we'll go across the lake,' I suggested. 'I spotted a canoe down there during the BBQ today. That's how we'll slip away.'

Melissa the moose bellowed softly. 'These woods are vast, but my herd knows them well. I can meet you on the other side of the lake, guide you through the forest to the nearest town.'

We went back to our tents and changed out of our PJs into more escape-from-crazy-cannibal-camp attire, which for me included a backpack of essentials (slow releasing energy snacks, first-aid kit, Sani-Gel) and a warm hoodie.

We slipped through the trees and found an overturned canoe and two paddles. I turned the canoe upright and, with Nesto's help, silently launched it into the water. Corina supervised.

I did my best to inspect it for spiders or any flesh-hungry insects, but Corina insisted that we deal with any creatures en route. She was right, it was only a few hours until sunup, and we needed to put as much distance between us and the camp as possible. I was convinced they'd come looking for us. I don't think Camp Nowannakidda would want their ingredients to escape.

As quietly as possible, Nesto and I paddled the canoe across the still lake until we beached on the soft sand of the western shore. I looked back to the waterfront of the camp and promised Amanda, 'I'll come back for you, sis.'

19

In Which We Get Our Moose On

Standing on the beach, I heard a whisper on the wind.

'Nesty and freaky friends, over here.'

I scanned the darkness beyond the beach, expecting a moose to nudge its huge head out of the woods. But instead, a girl with auburn hair, wearing a plaid dress, skipped onto the sand and gave Ernesto a moose-sized hug. Melissa.

'Isn't he cute?' asked Melissa, turning to us. 'I mean, I think I prefer him in scales, but this'll do too.'

I couldn't tell in the moonlight, but I think Ernesto was blushing. I looked at Corina and she looked paler than ever.

'I'm thinking about puking,' she said.

'You're right, Nesty,' said Melissa, 'she *is* frosty, even for a vampire.'

'You told her?' Corina asked.

'Don't worry, sister,' said Melissa. 'Nesty told me everything. About you, him, the neurotic zombie and that awful camp that wants to turn you all into doughnuts.'

Melissa led us deep into the woods, forging an expert path through the trees and bushes. 'You know,' she said, 'it's the same for our herd.'

'Moose doughnuts?' I asked.

'Now I will barf,' threatened Corina.

'More like steaks, fillets, burgers,' explained Melissa. 'Hunters come up to these woods and shoot us moose to put us on the menu.'

'You see,' said Corina. 'This is why I'm a vegan.'

'I like her,' said Melissa.

'She's pretty cool,' said Nesto.

'Frosty though?' said Corina.

'How 'bout you, Adam?' asked Melissa. 'You like Corina, don'cha?'

Like her? I was *crazy* about her. But I wasn't going to admit it or I'd never hear the end of it from the chatty chupacabra, sassy weremoose, or the sometimes vicious vampire in question.

'Yeah, I guess,' I said instead. 'Corina's nice.'

'That's the last thing I am, zom-brain,' scoffed Corina. 'If you can't say anything interesting, don't bother.'

'Awkward,' said Melissa, and she and Ernesto shared a giggle in front of us. They held hands and trudged through the forest, with Corina and me trailing behind.

'I didn't mean that,' I finally said to Corina. 'You're not nice, you're—'

'Oh, thanks for that,' she said.

'Whoa, no, what I meant was—'

'Zip it, zom-boy,' she said. 'Let's just get out of here, save the campers from the cannibals and get back to our normal lives as not-so-nice, nice monsters in hiding.'

'Wait, Corina, you're not a monster. You're super cool and sometimes that much coolness is hard to classify.'

'Really?' she asked, finally stopping to turn around.

'Yes, really,' I admitted. 'I think so, Nesto thinks so, all the kids at school think so, though they're too scared of you to admit it. The only "people" who don't seem to think so are your parents, so don't let their blindness stop you from seeing how great you are. You've been insanely hungry on this whole trip and you haven't even eaten one person. That's worthy of a greeting card!'

She threw her arms around me. I braced myself for lift-off.

'Where are we going?' I asked. But we didn't fly, we just stayed on the ground.

'I don't know,' said Corina, holding me tight. It was a real hug, not a form of transportation. Wow!

'Um, guys,' I heard Ernesto call.

'Hey, Nesty,' I called back, 'now *we're* having a moment.'

'Could use a little help here,' he replied.

Corina opened her arms and I looked over, then up, to see Nesto hanging in the air.

He was held up, tangled in the antlers of a very large, and very angry-looking moose.

'Daaad.' Melissa sighed. 'Put him down.'

20

In Which We Hit the Road

We were surrounded by muscly moose.* I counted at least ten and we had no obvious route for escape. Melissa was still in human-girl form, pleading with her father, and Ernesto was perched precariously on top of big papa's antlers.

'All humans are hunters,' the daddy moose grunted. 'And you are forbidden from cavorting with these ...' He snorted and took a good look at Corina and I. Then he sniffed us with his bulbous snout. '... What exactly are these ... creatures?'

'Chupacabra,' said Ernesto with a wave.

'Bless you,' said the papa moose.

'Isn't he sweet?' said Melissa. 'He's not a hunter. And he's got manners.'

---

* I've always thought the plural of 'moose' should be 'meese'.

The big moose shook his head (shaking Nesto inside the antler cage) and muttered under his breath. But he slowly lowered his head and Ernesto climbed off the antlers.

'We're different like you,' Nesto said. 'I'm a chupacabra, which is kinda like a Mexican weremoose, I think. And Adam here used to be human, but is now a zombie, but not the rampaging, flesh-eating kind. And Corina's a vampire.'

'Vegan,' she added.

'You have very strange friends, Melissa,' the alpha moose said. 'I'm worried their strangeness is contagious.'

'I'm helping them escape,' she said.

'The people who run the camp we were at,' I explained, 'are kind of like hunters. They trapped us inside and unless we stop them, they're going to turn the kids into food. We need to get far away from here, get to our parents and get help.'

The moose surrounding us all grunted and snorted.

'The herd will help,' said Melissa's father. 'We'll lead you as far south as we can.'

'That'd be great,' I said.

He crouched down and said, 'Melissa, climb on. You ride on me.'

Three other moose followed his lead. Nesto, Corina, and I each clambered onto a moose. It was time to travel in a pack, in a herd.

My moose was Melissa's uncle, Gordy, and he explained that the weremoose originated a bunch of years ago when radiation leaked from a nuclear plant way up north.

'My dad, Melissa's grandmoose, was innocently grazing when he wandered into some glowing sludge,' he explained. 'On the next full moon, much to his shock and surprise, he mutated into a person. Gramps never could choose between his life in the wild and life in the town, so he didn't. He led a type of double life, married the daughter of the town grocer, and started a herd of his own.'

I got the herd's whole story, from migration patterns to dodging hunters.

Aside from being full of doughnut-chomping cannibals and surprisingly friendly weremoose, my major observation of Canada was that it's a really, really big place.

I mean, I knew it was big from the TV weather map because it's where all of our bad weather comes from (cannibals plus cold snaps – that's two strikes against you, Canada!), but you only truly know how big a place is when you ride a moose for hours and hours through the woods.

'Are we there yet?' asked Nesto, pretty much every hour, on the hour.

Finally, up ahead, we heard the rush of the occasional car or truck. We pushed through the forest and found the main road.

'We leave you here,' said papa moose, whose name was Tom but insisted on being called sir.

'Thank you, sir,' I said, as the moose retreated from view.

'Bye, Melissa,' said Nesto.

'Bye, Nesty,' she said, joining her herd in the forest. But a moment later, she popped her head back out, in full moose mode, and added, 'Be careful, okay.'

With our moose escort gone, it was just the three of us at the side of the wilderness highway. Nesto immediately ignored Melissa's advice and walked to the tarmac and stuck out his hitchhiking thumb.

'Whoa,' I protested. 'Put that away.'

'Why?' he asked. 'No more moose. We need a lift.'

'We can't hitchhike. That's like asking to get abducted and murdered,' I said.

'You mean, abducted and murdered like we would be in the place we just escaped from?' asked Corina.

'Yes,' I agreed. 'There's no need to jump from the fire and into the frying pan.'

'Unless there's bacon in that frying pan,' said Nesto. He sniffed the air. 'Wait, I think there is.'

He turned his head southwards and sniffed the morning air. 'This way!'

We walked, single file, down the two-lane highway for about a mile, which is 2,042 steps (not that I was counting – okay, I was), until we found a roadside DINE (the R was broken) that boasted fresh mooseburgers.

'That's so wrong,' Ernesto fumed.

As we opened the glass doors to step inside, I noticed a plastic sign taped to the window: SOLD, Soon to be another Can Nibble Donut Shop.

The diner was bustling with clad-in-plaid locals and truckers topped in baseball caps that had nothing to do with baseball.

'Just take a seat where ya can find one, kids,' said a rotund, bearded man from the kitchen. He looked like Santa Claus in the off-season.

We took a booth. It was red plastic over a cushion, held together with strips of clear duct tape. Half of the lights were out and the black-and-white chequered floor was more like black and beige now. This place had seen better days.

But then again, so had I.

A chirpy woman in an apron and a name tag that read Shelly approached the booth with a coffee urn and pulled it back. 'You kids are too young for coffee.'

'Then I'll take theirs,' insisted Corina, not taking no for an answer. 'In fact, Shelly, you can just leave that right here.'

'Any food for you, boys and girl?' she asked.

'Not the mooseburger,' said Nesto. 'I'll have a plate of fries, Shelly.'

'Sorry, kid,' Shelly said. 'We don't cook lunch until eleven.'

'I'll take them raw,' he said.

'Frozen fries,' she jotted down.

'Can you put some gravy and cheese curds on them?' I asked.

Nesto looked at me like I was crazy.

'Trust me,' I said, turned back to our waitress. 'Grapefruit and muesli for me, and Corina's fine with the coffee.'

'Black as night, as sugary as candyland,' she ordered.

'Oh, and a milkshake,' added Nesto. 'With three straws.'

'Two,' said Corina.

'One,' I clarified. 'But I'd like a bottle of water. Bottled at the source, not a bottle that you fill up from the tap.'

Shelly rolled her eyes, which looked like it took a lot of effort. 'You kids have money to pay for all this?'

'Ooh,' said Nesto, shifting awkwardly on the bench.

'Don't worry,' I said. 'Mom gave me an advance on my allowance. Do you take American dollars?'

'More Yanks, eh?' she said. 'Just like them over there. You know 'em? Ha! Just kiddin', eh.'

I looked over at two truckers inhaling plates of eggs, bacon, and something that resembled toast. One wore a King-of-the-Road trucker cap and a T-shirt that boasted USA A-OK. The other guy was clad in plaid. I just hoped their driving skills were better than their fashion skills.

'Um, Shelly?' I said. 'Do you know which truck belongs to them?'

'The one with the logs,' she said, disappearing to log our order with Santa in the kitchen.

Outside, at least a dozen trucks were lined up in the parking lot, but only one had long rows of felled trees on its trailer.

'What are you thinking, zom-boy?' asked Corina.

'I'm thinking we just found our ride.'

21

In Which We Ride a Tree

We kept a close eye on the truckers and kept pace with their eating (which was hard) in a contest to the finish. As they were paying, I left a handful of bills on the table and we slipped out of the DINE and rushed towards the tree truck.

I noticed it had New York state plates, so although it wasn't Ohio, it was, at least, the right country. There was nobody we could talk to in Canada. I feared they were all complicit in their cannibal Can Nibble treats. We had to get stateside to talk to someone we could trust.

I pulled myself onto the back of the trailer and climbed up the horizontal logs. Of course, I was worried about splinters and insects, but I had to keep focused to reach the top of the pile. Nesto and Corina quickly followed and Nesto straddled a tree trunk like it was a pony.

'Giddy up, tree!' he said.

'Shhh,' I warned. 'Keep it down.'

'Is this safe?' asked Corina.

'Worrying about safety is my department,' I said. 'But if we're going to get to safety, this is our best bet. But please, hold on.'

Suddenly, a police car zoomed past, heading north, with its sirens blaring.

'Duck,' I said.

'Oooh, where?' asked Nesto.

I waved him down. 'Haven't you just eaten enough?'

'I don't know where my next meal's coming from. Excuse me for living.'

'And you want to keep living, right? If the camp leaders woke up this morning and noticed we're not there, they could hunt us down. We're fugitives.'

'Cool,' said Nesto.

'Actually, Adam, that is pretty cool,' agreed Corina.

The two truckers walked across the tarmac towards their cab.

'Flip ya for the wheel,' the King said.

'Nah, you take it. I wanna play on the CB.'*

---

* A CB is a Citizens Band radio, like a short-distance mobile phone used by truckers and people who really like to say 'ten-four'.

'So long as it's not Name That Tune,' complained King trucker.

Mr Plaid laughed. 'You spoil all the fun.'

The King jingled an enormous pile of keys in his hand. 'I'm thinkin' straight shot to the border, get some home cooking on American soil.'

'Amen, brother. Amen.'

The truck rumbled to life and pulled onto the two-lane highway. The wind swept our hair and the three of us did our best to stay low, crouching amid the timber.

It must have been the fresh air, the sleepless night, or the rhythmic rumbling of the semi-trailer, because I fell fast asleep.

*

The landscape around me was turquoise and vast. I was all alone, until out of the corner of my eye, I spotted something move. I turned around, but nothing.

Whoosh.

There it was again. And then behind me.

Suddenly, the smooth blue surface I was standing on, which reminded me of the kitchen counter at home, was overrun by slimy spheres, zipping and jumping all around me like kernels about to pop. I took a closer look – they were germs ... but they were alive with bulging eyes and jabbering mouths. I recognised them from my science textbook.

'Get away!' I shouted as salmonella slipped past me. 'Ick! Leave me alone.'

But the more agitated I got, the closer they came. A dozen E. coli ran rings around me, like a real-life 'ring-a-ring o' roses'. And I was going to be the one to *all fall down.*

The surface of this place, a planet perhaps, was now covered in germs. They spread and multiplied as far as I could see. And then something blocked out the light.

At first I thought it was a spaceship, white and angular. But as the strange ship got closer, I saw it for what it really was: a giant spray bottle.

A hand gripped the trigger and a spray showered from above.

'NO!' I shouted. 'I'm not one of them!'

But the antibacterial spray doused me and swept me away in a tumbling river of chemical cleanliness. The germs shouted and complained as we were all pushed off the flat surface of this strange world and down, down, down in an endless waterfall cascade of cleaning product.

'Adam,' called a voice, a girl's voice. Corina's voice. 'Adam.'

And suddenly I was somewhere else.

*

'I don't want to be cleaned away!' I shouted.

'You were dreaming, Adam,' said Corina, as my eyesight readjusted to our treetop trailer. We were stationary and I could smell the fumes of idling traffic combined with something else – a fresh mist in the air.

'You were freakin' out,' said Ernesto. 'It was awesome!'

'Where are we?' I asked, groggily.

'You're not going to believe it,' said Corina. 'Look.'

I slowly raised my head and looked down, instantly regretting it. Below, far below, was nothing but raging water. I shook and trembled.

'Easy there, zom-boy,' said Corina, calmly. 'Look.'

I glanced around and saw that the truck was in a line of traffic high above a river on a very long bridge. And then I saw the source of the mist: Niagara Falls.

The water rushed over the horseshoe-shaped cliff to our right. Water vapour billowed into the sky, clouding

140

out the sun and creating a triple-rainbow bridge over the gap that separated the two countries.

I'd been here before, when I was in second grade, on one of Mom and Dad's epic road trips. We stayed in a motel that had more mice than guests, and we lined up along the edge of the Falls to watch some daredevil barrel over in a ... well, barrel. It was one of those things that adults did because it was there – tempting death with feats of stupidity. On the plus side, there was ice cream.

'We're on the bridge between cannibal land and Home of the Brave,' said Corina.

I looked back at the start of the bridge and spotted the Canadian flag flying next to the stars and stripes. I exhaled, a sigh of relief. 'We made it.'

'Not quite,' said Corina, pointing to the checkpoint up ahead. The American border police were checking every car, every truck, every passenger. Two uniformed guards held mirrors on sticks, checking the undercarriages of trucks and cars for things that shouldn't be there. And they were looking on top of every truck. I didn't know if there was an illegal immigration issue from Canada, but these zealous border guards weren't letting anyone in without a passport.

Which we didn't have.

'It'll be fine,' I said. 'We're Americans returning home and we'll just explain everything to the guards.'

But Nesto shook his head and looked more scared than when I told him we were destined to be turned into doughnuts. 'But what if I'm not American?'

'You're, like, fourth-generation American,' I reminded him. 'That makes you as American as apple pie, or at least apple tacos.'

He shook his head urgently. 'No, I just tell everyone that. I was born in Guadalajara and my parents smuggled me in when I was a baby. That passport I have is a fake. It's a really good fake, but without it . . .'

'If they find him, they will deport him,' said Corina. 'You know that, right?'

The truck rumbled forward, inching towards the border . . . and the border control. I couldn't let my friend get caught.

'C'mon,' I urged. 'Let's get down.'

'Not down there!' Nesto said, pointing to the raging river below.

'Well, not yet,' I said. 'There's more than one way to cross the border.'

I pointed to the Horseshoe Falls. Masses of water rushed over the falls, sending a plume of mist high into the sky. The water poured into the lower Niagara River, which washed up onto the north shore of the United States.

That's when it came to me, an idea for how to sneak into our homeland.

22

In Which We Sneak Back into Canada

We clambered off the trailer and, crouching down, weaved though the idling cars, quickly and silently slipping back into Canada.

'I think Adam's brain has fully decomposed,' said Ernesto.

'I can't believe I'm agreeing with you,' said Corina.

As we approached the Canadian border, a uniformed man with a bushy moustache that nearly covered his mouth held up his hand to stop us. 'Where are you kids going?'

'We have to pee really, really bad,' I said. It actually wasn't a lie. I needed to go.

'All of you?' asked the moustache.

Nesto crossed his legs and did a pee dance. 'I can't hold it,' he said.

He unzipped his fly and made to let his little chup loose.

'Whoa, whoa, whoa,' he said. 'The bathrooms are at the back of that building. Get going and then get back in your parents' car. You're on Canadian soil now and we're not a toilet.'

We ran behind the building . . . and kept on running. The traffic was near a standstill approaching the bridge, and we cut across a green field and then along the road overlooking the roaring Niagara River.

'Nice acting, Nesto,' said Corina.

But then he stopped at a tree and unzipped his shorts for real. 'C'mon, Adam, sword fight!'

'Uggh,' Corina grunted as she looked away.

'I can hold mine,' I said, not totally sure that I could.

As Ernesto watered the tree, a lady wearing shiny, tight-fitting running gear jogged by while pulling her golden retriever on a leash. Upon seeing Nesto, the dog tugged his athletic owner over and lifted his leg.

'Get your own tree,' hissed Ernesto.

Woof woof.

The dog barked, defending what it clearly thought was its territory.

The lady removed her ear buds and looked at us. 'You really shouldn't let your friend pee in public.'

My hypocrisy alarm went off.

'Tell that to your dog,' I said. 'It's spraying bacteria and germs all over the place.'

'It's what dogs do,' she said. As if that were an excuse.

Suddenly, the pooch *yelped* with fright.

Out of the corner of my eye I noticed that Nesto had chupafied his face. The quick change from prepubescent boy to lizard face shocked the dog and it pulled its owner away.

Nesto shook off his chupa look and calmly put away his watering hose.

'Wow,' I said. 'I've never seen you do that before.'

'Well, if you can't pee in front of your friends then who—' started Nesto.

'Actually,' I interrupted, leading us along the pathway towards the roaring Falls. 'I meant the quick change into chupa. That was pretty amazing.'

'Oh, yeah. I'm getting better at controlling it. I was practising with Melissa.'

We kept walking along the river until we reached the throngs of gaping tourists marvelling at one of the wonders of the world. The water rushed right past them as we, three *monstrous* wonders, walked among them. It did briefly make me wonder how many people would come to see us if we were ever caught and put on display? How much would the tickets go for? How long would the lines be?

'Adam,' snapped Corina. 'Where are we going?'

'To get our ride,' I said.

I led them through the busy crowd and across the street to the Niagara Falls Museum.

I still had some money, so I bought us three tickets to a glimpse into Niagara's past. We whizzed through the rooms about the native Canadians, first explorers, geological make-up of the area (bedrock granite) until we reached the daredevil display.

There was a tightrope above us with a mannequin balanced on it. Below, photos showed Charles Blondin, a French guy who was the first person to tightrope walk across the Niagara gorge. Next, we found a life-sized photo of Annie Edson Taylor, an old lady who, at 63, was the very first person to survive a trip over the falls. And then, around the corner, we found what I was looking for: a modern-day barrel.

It was silver and sleek, like a slice of a rocket.

'That's our ride home, guys,' I announced.

'It looks heavy,' said Nesto.

'You know I could just fly you over the river,' suggested Corina.

'Over one of the world's most watched tourist attractions?' I asked. 'You'd be a YouTube sensation in seconds.'

'I could tunnel underneath,' offered Nesto.

'Didn't you pay attention?' I asked. 'Niagara is built on bedrock. I know you've got razor-sharp claws, but I think we'd need dynamite to bust our way in and somehow I don't think that'd lead to a warm welcome.'

'Okay, zom-boy, how do we roll out this barrel of fun?'

'Exactly,' I said. 'Give me a hand.'

'This is insane,' Corina said, nonetheless lending me two pale hands to push the barrel off its display.

Nesto guided the silver cylinder towards the double doors at the back as Corina and I rolled it quickly, but deliberately.

'Where are you going with that?' called a voice.

I peeked around the barrel to see a bored-looking teenager wearing a uniform and name tag entering the daredevil room. He held a walkie-talkie and was about to use it to radio in our barrel theft.

We were done for.

I noticed Corina's fangs extend and I held her back. 'Wait, not yet.'

She was clearly considering giving in to her hunger. But instead of letting her, I eyed the guard's name tag and tried to reason with him.

'Bernie,' I said. 'Before you call anyone on that, we've got one heck of a story to tell you.'

'Does it involve me getting fired?' he asked.

'Probably,' I said, 'but at least you'll get to see something I bet you've never seen before.'

'You're going over the falls, aren't you?' he asked.

'Bernie, we may look like ordinary kids to you—'

'You don't actually, you all look a bit, well—'

'Different?' I asked. He nodded his head. I decided that faced with being stopped, and then arrested, for stealing an artefact from the museum, our best way out was the truth. Nobody would believe the truth. 'We are different. And now we're going to show you just how different.'

'Really?' asked Nesto.

'Is this a good idea, zom-boy?'

'Bernie, I'm a zombie, Corina here is a vampire, and Ernesto is a . . .'

Suddenly, Nesto transmutated and Corina revealed her fangs. Bernie leapt back.

'Is this a trick?' he asked.

'The only trick,' I said, 'is that we're taking this barrel and going to make it disappear. If you try to stop us, my hungry vampire friend will feed on you. And Nesto may later chew on your bones. He likes bone.'

Bernie froze, trembling and nearly hyperventilating. Finally, he spoke.

'Awesome,' he uttered.

'Huh?' I grunted.

'I've worked here for three summers,' he said, 'and I've never seen anyone actually go over the Falls. I'm going to record the whole thing on my phone.'

'Awesome,' I agreed.

23

In Which We Have a Barrel of Fun (Invading America)

We literally stopped traffic pushing the barrel across the road, but nobody official stopped us. A few tourists snapped photos on their phones, but that was the extent of the attention we attracted. Slowly, we pushed the aluminium barrel along the sidewalk, upriver, until we reached a small park overlooking the rushing water.

We moved it as close as we could to the edge and Corina snapped the steel barrier fence with her bare hands.

'Roller coaster's open,' she said with a grin. 'And you've got to be this high to ride.'

She held her hand out level with the ground, at shoulder height. Nesto rushed over. He stood under her palm on his tippy-toes, pushing his head against her hand.

'All right,' he said. 'I'm never big enough at the state fair!'

I climbed up the barrier and on top of the barrel.

'This isn't going to be like anything they've got there,' I said, turning the wheel to open the hatch, and peering inside.

The chamber inside was dank and dark, with straps and cushions, but only built for one man. I hoped that since Ernesto was so small, and I wasn't exactly being invited into professional wrestling, we could all fit.

'Nesto, you and Corina hop in and I'll go last.'

Ernesto clambered up and then down into the chamber. 'It smells in here.'

'Smells like fear,' Corina said, floating herself down and finding a strap to hold on to.

'It's going to be a rough ride,' I said. 'But we can take it.'

I lowered myself into the dark chamber and sealed us in. It was pitch-black since I hadn't thought to find the interior light.

'All right, guys, now push on the wall.'

At once, we all pushed in different directions.

Booof.

We slammed into one another.

'Let's try that again,' I said. 'Okay, put your hands in the middle, and then swing and push the way my hand leads.'

Everyone popped their hands on mine and I counted to three before moving my hand in the direction of the river shore.

We tilted, but didn't topple.

'Okay, again!' I called.

Still no movement.

'One more time,' I urged.

With a heave, we slowly toppled over, and over, and over, until we bounced into the water. I could feel the wave bob us up and down, like my rubber duck in the bath.

'So this is nice,' said Corina.

'Thanks for getting me off the bridge,' said Ernesto.

'We weren't going to risk you getting deported,' I said.

Corina laughed. 'He's willing to risk your untimely death in an aluminium can going over a massive waterfall, but deportation ... nah, that's a risk he just won't take.'

'I didn't hear any better ideas,' I said. 'Besides, this is me trying to relax. Have either of you—'

And then my stomach jumped into my throat.

'Wheeeee!' squealed Ernesto.

My head was upside down. Then sideways, then pressed into Ernesto's stinky armpit.

We tumbled and tossed and plummeted. I had no

idea what was going on, but I now knew what my clothes felt like when I put them in the dryer.

'Maybe we should have just flooooooooown,' I said, just as the barrel slammed into the water below. But the tumbling didn't stop. We rocked and turned until finally the shaking stopped.

'Can we get out now?' asked Ernesto.

'Wait 'til we've come to a full and complete stop.'

'Adam,' said Corina. 'What if we bank on the Canadian side of the river?'

'I think that's when we move to the power of flight. Maybe you could drag Nesto and me across the river – make it look like we're swimming?'

'Fine,' she said with a huff.

Finally, we stopped moving and the barrel keeled over onto one side . . . my side.

Nesto and Corina flopped on top of me.

'Ouch, careful of the cartilage,' I said.

'I guess we've landed,' said Nesto. I reached over to the side and turned the locking wheel. I pulled myself out and onto the sandy bank of the river. At first, I couldn't see which side of the border we'd landed on. As I stood up, an unfriendly, but distinctly American, voice told me to put my, 'Hands up!'

I turned to see my own double reflection in a policeman's mirrored sunglasses.

'I'm so glad to see you,' I said.

'I'm about to arrest you for illegal stunting over the border – I wouldn't be that glad, son,' he said.

Nesto crawled out of the barrel, followed by Corina.

'Any more?' the cop asked.

'Just us,' said Corina, rubbing her head.

Nesto twitched nervously. I could tell he was nervous about risking deportation.

'What's going on here, kids?' he asked. 'And tell me the truth.'

'Officer,' I began, 'the truth is we escaped Canada, a nation of doughnut-munching cannibals. We were at a camp that turns kids into doughnuts, and we got out to get help because there's almost sixty more fine Americans left behind.'

'Good God.' He trembled, took off his glasses and crouched down to our level. 'It's just like 'Nam.'

'You were in Vietnam?' I asked.*

---

* Vietnam is a country in South East Asia that grown-ups like to go to on holiday. But before I was born, America fought a big war there and not even my history teacher is sure why.

'Yeah, last year the missus and I were on holiday there and, well, let's just say that the all-inclusive resort didn't include much. We got out but left some good people behind. I said I'd alert the travel agent and go back for them, but ... but we never did.'

'What happened to them?' Nesto asked.

'Never saw them again,' the cop said, hanging his head. 'But a few weeks later I noticed on TripAdvisor that a few of them posted pretty nasty reviews. I don't think they had a good holiday: unclean sheets, unruly staff, and drinks watered down ... with dirty water.'

'Sounds like Hell,' I said.

'It was,' the cop replied, starting to tear up. 'And I never went back.'

'But it's not too late for our friends,' said Corina. 'Will you help us?'

The cop stood up and exhaled, breathing out his guilt. 'I will. What do you need?'

'We need a ride to Croxton, Ohio,' I said.

'That, I can do,' he said.

24

In Which We Return Home

We were crammed into the back seat (behind the steel divider) of Officer Campbell's patrol car for about seven hours of interstate driving. Officer Campbell, whose first name was Bob (not short for Robert, but Bobert . . . his parents misspelled his birth certificate), was actually a really nice guy, had three kids slightly younger than us, and a penchant for show tunes.

Bobert and I sang our way across upstate New York, north Pennsylvania, and into good ol' Ohio. Either he was tone-deaf or just very polite, but either way, he didn't arrest me for being hopelessly out of tune. Corina and Nesto, however, were not so kind. They pleaded with me to stop, but sometimes, and being locked in the back of a police car with a vampire and a chupacabra is one of those times, you just gotta sing!

He used the red-and-blue lights so we made good time,

stopping for only three 'comfort' breaks which weren't all that comfortable given that they involved very well-used urinals. He offered to buy us snacks and lunch, and none of us were tempted by anything resembling a doughnut.

We'd finally reached my parents on the cop's phone and reassured them that we'd escaped from the cannibals and were going to bust Amanda out when we returned. My dad had laughed and assumed I was joking, which was probably all for the best.

We finally rolled into Croxton just before dusk, cruising down Main Street in an out-of-state cruiser, and found our hometown totally empty and eerily quiet. We asked Officer Campbell to take us to Corina's place.

'The town feels deserted,' I said.

'Ooh, more dessert for us,' Nesto chirped, hopefully.

Most of the townsfolk had rented out their homes for extraordinary rents and taken holidays. The dentist vampires had moved in and now, late in the afternoon, many of them would still be in their coffins.

'Twenty-nine Holmcrest Road?' asked Officer Campbell. 'We're here.'

We piled out of the cop car and thanked him for bringing us home.

'If you ever need anything kids, this is my card,' he

said, handing Corina a small piece of white cardboard. 'But, first, I'd like a word with your parents.'

'That's probably not a good idea,' said Corina.

'I insist,' he said, friendly but firm.

Corina reached under the decrepit-looking garden gnome on her front porch, grabbed the spare key and unlocked her front door. The vampire invited us inside.

She led us through the front hall to the kitchen, which looked like a display model at IKEA and had probably cooked as many meals. 'I can offer you tap water,' she said, 'and that's about it.'

'Water's fine,' Bob confirmed, gulping the liquid that had once passed through the sewage treatment plant. I tensed, thinking about all the contaminants he was consuming.

'Corina? Is that you?' called Corina's mother from the curved stairway at the front. 'What in Count's name are you doing—'

'We have *visitors*, Mother,' Corina called back.

Corina's mom swept into the kitchen, wearing a flowing black gown.

'Ma'am,' said Officer Campbell.

Corina's mother stroked the cop's shoulder and sniffed him.

'What have you brought me, daughter?'

Corina shook her head.

'This is Officer Campbell and he helped us,' she explained. 'When we escaped from the camp you sent us to, which was actually run by an evil witch.'

She blinked twice. 'And the problem is?'

'She's fattening up the campers and turning them into doughnuts,' Corina said.

'And then the Canadians eat the doughnuts,' I added. 'They're all cannibals.'

'Which is downright unAmerican,' Officer Campbell stated. 'And these kids unearthed the whole cruel conspiracy.'

Mrs Parker looked at the policeman in her kitchen and licked her lips. 'You've brought us a treat, Corina.'

'Can I have some?' asked Nesto. 'Adam promised me dessert.'

Corina's mom rolled her eyes. 'I see that my daughter is running in packs now.'

Nesto grinned. 'We're more like a little herd.'

Officer Campbell cleared his throat nervously. 'I just wanted to be sure that a responsible adult was present. And I can see you all have some family business to catch up on. Corina, Adam, Ernesto, it's been a pleasure, and please be sure you alert your local authorities to get your friends back. And good day to you, ma'am.'

He turned to leave, escaping the Parker house of horrors.

'Well that's a pity,' said Mrs Parker. 'I haven't had breakfast.'

'*You* scared him off,' huffed Corina, 'and he's a nice man who helped us. I think he deserves to live.'

'Well, that's a pity,' she said, 'because I haven't chosen my sacrifice yet.'

'What are you talking about, Mother?' asked Corina.

'Oh you know,' she began, looking suspiciously at Nesto and me, 'just dentist stuff. Nothing to concern yourself with.'

I heard their front door open and a man's voice called out, 'I'm back!'

'Speak of the dentist,' Mrs Parker said.

It was Corina's one-armed dentist father, Dr Parker. 'But why is there a New York State law enforcement officer in our driveway?'

'Because he's not in a cage,' sulked Mrs Parker.

Dr Parker strode into the kitchen wearing full running gear. Taking no notice of us, he headed straight to the fridge and cracked open a blood-flavoured

Vampade drink. He stretched his calves by pressing against the fridge door, huffing and puffing.

'How many times?' exclaimed Corina's mom. 'No stretching in the kitchen.'

'You don't want me seizing up, do you?' asked Dr Parker, finally turning around. 'Corina?' he gasped. 'What in Count's name are you doing home from camp?'

'Cannibals, Canadians, doughnuts,' she explained.

'Got it,' he said, though I wasn't sure he actually did. 'Well I'm glad you're back. You're just in time for the big event tonight. But I'm surprised by your choice offerings. Hello, boys.'

'No,' said Corina, 'these are my friends. They're off limits.'

I raised my hand like I was still in seventh grade. 'Um, what are you guys talking about?'

'Private dental matter, Adam,' he said.

'They know,' Corina said to her parents, 'all about us.'

Dr Parker dropped his smile. 'Well, that's very unfortunate for them.'

'Easy, Dad, they're not human. They're *unnatural* ... just like us.'

'Watch your mouth, offspring!' snapped Corina's mom.

'They're not vampires,' said Dr Parker, stroking his chin. 'Werewolves?'

Nesto hung his head and sighed. He took a quick breath and burst into chupa mode from the neck up. His skin turned to scales and his teeth sprouted fangs. His bulbous black eyes reflected the curious looks of Corina's vamparents. Nesto switched back just as fast.

'A werewolf with a fur problem,' mused Dr Parker.

'No, chupacabra,' said Ernesto, rolling his now-human eyes.

'Never heard of it,' the dentist admitted. 'Though I would like to investigate that mouth for fang decay.'

'I don't weally like wentists,' mumbled Nesto, keeping his mouth tightly shut.

'None taken,' said Dr Parker. 'But what about you, Adam? Are you a chupachup too?'

'Zombie, actually,' I said.

'You don't look much like a zombie,' said Corina's mom, dismissively.

'Thanks,' I said.

'Hey, Adam,' said Nesto. 'Do the walk and maybe a groan.'

I didn't want play into stereotypes, but I did want them to believe I was as unnatural as they were. I lifted my arms in front of me, shuffled across the tile floor, and even groaned for effect.

'Ah, I see it now, ' said Mrs Parker, then turning to Corina she continued, 'Your friends may be *unnatural*, as you say, but they are nothing like us. We are Count's divine creatures, and these boys are, well, abominations.'

Nesto tugged my sleeve. 'Is that a good thing or a bad thing?'

'That's not very nice,' I said to Corina's mom.

'I'm not a very nice person,' she replied, echoing something Corina had said to me when we first met. As much as Corina wanted to distance herself from Mommy Fearest, there was an apple/tree thing going on.

'No, Mother,' said Corina, 'sacrifice isn't very *nice*.'

'It's tradition,' said Dr Parker with a shrug, the way my dad might refer to Thanksgiving dinner.

'I'm sorry,' I said. 'Who's sacrificing who?'

'It's an ancient tradition,' explained Dr Parker. 'The vampires assemble every four years and sacrifice those who have affronted our community.'

'I always thought that was just a bedtime story,' said Corina.

'Doesn't mean it isn't real,' said her mom. 'It's been

going on since before humans walked the Earth. What do you think happened to the dinosaurs?'

I'd always assumed the death of the dinosaurs was at the hands (or claws) of their bad food hygiene, not bloodsucking, ritualistic vampires.

'It's the natural order of things – every vampire gets to make a sacrifice,' said Dr Parker. 'We are superior beings and it's important to remind ourselves, and others, of that fact.'

'*Opinion*,' said Corina pointedly. 'This is so typical. The vampires just do whatever they want.'

'Don't be disloyal, child,' snapped Mrs Parker.

'Like kill off the dinosaurs,' said Ernesto, shaking his head in shock.

'It's not right,' said Corina in a huff. 'You can't just sacrifice people to make yourselves feel better.'

'We knew you wouldn't understand, dear,' said Dr Parker. 'But the sacrifice is an important part of our culture. It's the one time a vampire can stand up in front of all other vampires and, well, be himself.'

'IS THAT WHY YOU SENT ME AWAY?' Corina shouted.

'These affairs are above you, dear,' said her mom.

Nesto looked up as Corina sighed. I turned to my

friend, the vegan vampire, and urged her to act. 'If every vampire gets to make a sacrifice, you can talk to them all, change their minds.'

But her mom blurted a sarcastic laugh. 'Don't be absurd, flesheater. Nobody listens to her.'

Corina shrank just a little bit, hung her head and looked at the floor. I hated the way her parents couldn't see how awesome she was. It clearly got to Corina because she stormed out the front door. I'm pretty sure I spotted her mascara running.

'It's not absurd,' I said in my friend's defence. 'And I never eat flesh, unlike some people I could mention . . . And people do listen to Corina because she's amazing. And she's going to stop this stupid tradition. Tonight!'

I motioned to Ernesto and we both bolted from the Parker home to find our friend.

25

In Which We Get Vampiric!

From the Parker's front yard I caught a glimpse of Corina soaring across the early evening sky.

'She's going to be seen,' fretted Ernesto. I wondered if my worrying nature was beginning to rub off on my friends.

'By who? Just a bunch of vampires waking up, getting ready to murder people they think are inferior,' I said. 'C'mon, I think I know where she's going.'

Nesto and I walked down the street, around two corners, and entered the forest surrounded by houses. It was getting darker now and the setting sun flickered through the leaves, giving the forest a blue tinge in some parts and a rippling burnt orange in others.

'Corina!' I called up to the treetops.

'Go away,' she yelled back.

'Your parents are idiots,' I said.

I spotted Corina perching on a tall branch of an oak tree. 'Of course they are,' she said. 'They're parents. That's their job. And my parents are just really, really good at it.'

Nesto shivered and shook, his light-brown skin popped yellowish-green scales and he let out a fast rip of a *roar*. He pounced onto all fours and looked back at me. His face was completely chupafied, but his clothes were still on. He was getting really good at transformation. For a brief moment, I was jealous that he could switch back and forth so easily.

'Climb on,' he urged.

'Um.' I hesitated. 'You mean like *touching* you?'

'Hop on, Adam. It's the fastest way.'

I climbed on his back and wobbled uneasily as he trotted towards the tree.

'I'd really like a seat belt with a five-point harness,' I said. 'And a helmet.'

Nesto stood on his hind legs and clawed at the tree with his front claws. I leaned forward and held onto him as we quickly rose up the tree trunk. Leaves and small branches slapped me in the face as we climbed.

'Can you watch where you're going, Nesto?'

'Can you be grateful for the lift?' he asked back.

'Fair enough,' I admitted.

Finally, we reached the branch where Corina was sitting. She pushed off and floated in the air as if to fly away.

'Wait,' I asked, as I clutched onto the safety of the branch. 'Has this been load-tested?'

'I'm outta here,' she said.

I walked closer along the ever-thinning branch. I could feel it dip down, but as much as I wanted to turn back, I knew she needed us. 'Corina, we need you. Everyone needs you'

'Not my parents.'

'Then move in with me,' I offered. 'My parents already like you more than they like me.'

'They wouldn't if I sucked their blood dry.'

Yes, I thought, *that would tip me back into their favour.*

'Obviously,' I said. 'But I know and you know, and they don't need to know, that you're not going to do that.'

'Why are you so sure. I'm hungry all the time. I can feel it consuming me, taking over. This sacrifice they're having tonight, there's a part of me, a big part, that wants to join in.'

Nesto climbed a bit closer and perched beside me. We both faced Corina, floating before us. 'I feel it too, you know.'

'A hunger?' I asked.

'Not exactly,' Nesto said. 'I don't really know what to call it, but an urge maybe. I fight it all the time. I know sometimes you guys think I'm just kidding around and being silly, but that's what helps to keep my mind off it. When I'm quiet, especially at night, I just, well, I just need to be the monster. I need to thrash, destroy, eat prey and fend off predators.'

'How do you control it?' asked Corina.

'I didn't used to, not very well,' he said.

'My mom's flowers can attest to that,' I said.

'But you know,' he continued, 'since I started hanging out with you guys, it's become a lot better. I feel almost like I've got power over it, and not the other way around. I think it's because I'm friends with you. I've never really had friends before, just too many brothers and sisters. But now that I feel part of something, I know I'm not just a monster, I'm a person too. And so are you, Corina. And that's why you have to try to stop

170

the vampires. Because even though we're weird and monsters and all that, we're people too. And people should *not* be sacrificed.'

Corina floated a bit higher, gazing over the town. The tall spires of the university jutted up into the dusk sky.

'They'll be assembling now,' she said. 'And Dad said that every vampire gets to present their offering.'

'Do you think you could talk to them all?' I asked.

'I can try,' she said softly.

'And we'll cheer you on,' said Nesto.

'That's probably not a good idea,' she said. 'This is a vampire-only convention. This is something I've got to do alone.'

I didn't doubt that Corina could do it, but once inside, surrounded by her own kind, especially her unkind parents, I knew she'd need a friend or two.

'If we can sneak into America in a barrel,' I said, 'I'm sure we can get into a vampire pow-wow. Right?'

She shook her head. 'The only way they'd ever let you in is as—'

Corina froze, looking conflicted and afraid. She turned from us with a distant and faraway look. I mean, more far away than her normal bored, disinterested demeanour.

'The only way they'd ever let you in is as ... my *sacrifice*.'

I was suddenly sorry I asked.

26

In Which I Get Caged

Corina ripped the chains off the park's swing set.

'That's vandalism,' I pointed out. 'Not just illegal, but also very uncommunity-like.'

'Yeah,' added Nesto, 'and that swing went the highest.'

'Hold still,' she ordered, wrapping one of the chains around Nesto's arms and then all over his upper body. 'I think we can sacrifice one swing.'

'When you put it that way,' I said.

She bound my arms in the chains and spun me around, wrapping me in a chain-link cocoon. At once I was both terrified about what was about to happen and excited to be so close to Corina. I inhaled her clinical-smelling, grapefruit-infused scent.

Corina pulled the chains tighter. 'What did I say about smelling me?'

'I have to breathe,' I said in my defence. 'I can't help it if you're right in front of my nose.'

'Yeah me too,' said Nesto. 'Can I smell you too?'

'Breathe through your mouth and don't talk. Just listen,' she ordered. 'I grew up with bedtime stories of "The Sacrifice" . . .'

'Soothing,' I said.

'Just listen,' she repeated. 'I always assumed it was just a myth, but in the story vampires get to bring anyone they choose. Usually it's people that annoy you, like anyone who cut Mom off in traffic. My dad used to boast about catching telemarketers who called during breakfast time. I never really believed them, but I guess it's all true. In the stories, the ritual is always the same. You bring the human, introduce their crime to the community, and then let the guests feed. It's supposed to be one victim per vampire, but since you guys are small, maybe I can make a case for two.'

'Thanks,' said Nesto. 'Wait, no. How 'bout you just take Adam since he really likes you. He'd totally die for you. You know . . . if he could.'

'I'm not that small,' I protested.

'Shut it, zom-boy,' said Corina, 'and follow my lead.'

All tied up, she flew us to Convocation Hall, the

university's biggest building. It was a giant arched cathedral that held thousands of people to sit exams and, after sitting through enough exams, get their diplomas.

Hundreds of vampires, wearing name tags, filed into the building. They buzzed and gossiped excitedly. Some of them were leading blindfolded and muzzled humans on leashes, and Corina followed this crowd towards the back of the Hall.

A pale lady wearing a headset and clutching a clipboard was checking-in the vamps and taking down details of the victims in tow. Just ahead of us, she checked in a 'dentist' going by the name of Doctor Barry Kolchak who presented his human for inspection.

'And how has this human affronted you or our kind?'

'He had seventeen items,' explained Dr Kolchak, 'in the "Ten Items Or Less" line at the supermarket checkout.'

'Fewer,' I said, correcting his grammar. Corina gave me a kick.

'Barbaric,' cussed the clipboard lady to Dr Kolchak. 'These humans are so ... inhuman. You may proceed and happy sacrifice. Next!'

Corina yanked us forward.

'Where's your convention badge?' asked the lady.

'It doesn't go with my outfit,' Corina said.

'Then how do I know you're part of our esteemed dentist community?'

Corina let go of our chains and rose up into the air about three feet.

'That'll do,' the lady said. 'Full name?'

'Corina Adina Parker.'

'Your middle name rhymes?' I gasped.

The lady looked sternly at Corina. 'Your offering may not speak.'

'Sorry about that. Hear that offering . . . you may not speak.'

The clipboard lady examined Nesto and me. 'And aside from this one being weird-looking and the small one having an abundance of dirt under his fingernails . . . behind his ears . . . and, oh my Count, in his hair, why are these humans worthy of sacrifice?'

'This one stole my make-up and the little one doesn't wash his hands after relieving himself.'

'Despicable, both of them. In you go. Happy sacrifice!'

'You too,' said Corina with a smile, pulling us through the door into a corridor where the other humans were being caged like animals. Two hulking vampires grabbed me and tossed me into a large dog cage. I saw Nesto similarly manhandled, but instead of falling in with a thud, he pounced into what actually looked like a snug little room for him.

'Corina, what's going on?' I asked.

'They won't touch you until I call you onto the stage, I think,' she explained. I just hoped her memory of gruesome bedtime stories was accurate.

'So I'm at the mercy of their rule-following until then?'

"Fraid so,' she said. 'But my uncle's kind of a big deal around here, so I'll find him and get up there, first. Until then, just make yourself comfortable.'

'I kinda am,' said Nesto, curled up like a sleeping dog.

One of the guards banged on the cage. 'The offering may not speak.'

'Fine with me,' said Nesto. 'I'm going to take a nap.'

'How can you sleep at a time like this?' I snapped. But he was already snoring.

I looked up as Corina disappeared through the crowd. My cage was lifted onto a dolly – not a cuddly doll, but, like, a large skateboard – and I was whisked away, behind the slumbering chupacabra, into a dark room, caged like a beast ready for human sacrifice.

I kind of wish we'd stayed at camp.

27

In Which I Make My Vampire Debut

I couldn't see anything, but I could hear it all. Alone in the dark, in what I guessed was the on-deck circle[*] of death and dismemberment, I listened as a vampire roused the crowd with his speech.

'Friends, vampires! We have travelled from all over the world to be together, to come out of the shadows and celebrate.

'We assemble like this through the centuries, through good times and bad, but the restoration of kinship of our kind gives us the strength to live among the humans in the knowledge that we are not

---

[*] I guess some of that baseball game stuck with me. The on-deck circle is the area where the next batter up to the plate warms up by swinging the bat. In my case, I think I was next up to be presented for 'sacrifice'. It made me think much more fondly about baseball.

alone. We are part of something bigger, something greater.

'And hasn't it been great so far? This year's skull-tossing contest has been the best yet, and from the craftsmanship of the coffin building, I know that tradition isn't going to fade away in this century! I'm still licking my lips from the blood smoothies we enjoyed yesterday. It's been good times.

'And tonight, we continue our celebrations with the glorious tradition of sacrifice!'

The hall erupted in cheers and it felt like the bricks were rumbling. The vampire spoke with such conviction about something so terrible. At first, I couldn't understand how anyone would listen to him, let alone cheer for him, but as he spoke I realised he possessed such confidence that weaker minds would flock to his strength.

'We reassert our superiority through sacrifice. And I'm delighted to see the youth of our kind are so energetic about such old traditions. So this evening, we'll begin with one of our youngest, a local vamp from right here in Croxton, Ohio. Corina Parker.'

I didn't know what Corina planned to say to counter such a rally, or even if she could, but I knew I had to help her somehow.

Suddenly, amid the dying applause, a light brightened the holding cell. I was wheeled out onto a shiny black stage. I looked up, but I was briefly blinded by the spotlights.

'Who's making all that noise?'

I looked to my right, and Nesto was waking grumpily in his cage.

'Hi guys,' said Corina. She stood centre stage as Nesto and I were wheeled in on either side of her. 'I'm Corina . . . as you already know.' She seemed nervous, a bit unsure of herself. 'And I'm really hungry.'

The crowd clapped, clearly agreeing with her.

'But I'm a vegan,' she shared. The crowd immediately turned on her, booing her meat-free diet. 'Or at least, I used to be. A few weeks ago I had my first taste of human blood in a very long time.'

The vampires exploded into applause, but then seemed confused . . .

'And I haven't been able to stop thinking about it since. So I know how you feel. And I just got back from a place where I was cooped up with a bunch of humans. We were literally trapped, but they were trapped with me. And part of me wanted to taste every last one of them. And the only thing that stopped me was my friends. And I brought them to meet you today . . .'

There was a nervous laugh from the room as Corina opened my cage.

I heard a few in the crowd chant, 'Sacrifice' and 'Offering'.

Together we opened Nesto's cage and he pounced out. She held our hands and walked back to the front of the stage. With us at her sides, I noticed she stood a little taller.

'These aren't ordinary humans,' she said above the chanting. 'My friends are *different*, just like we are different.'

She looked at Nesto, and then at me. 'Show them.'

Nesto threw forth his arms and jumped onto all fours.

'Ernesto looks human, right?' asked Corina. 'Look again.'

As Nesto's hands hit the ground, they turned into claws. His tale sprung out of his shorts and his skin shimmered in a cascade of scales. He opened his jaw, displaying his fangs, and let out a roar that deafened the protesting chants.

'And this is Adam. Underneath his caked-on

make-up, is grey, brittle flesh that's unnaturally resilient to death.'

I grabbed an antibac wipe from my pocket and removed the make-up from my face. Before thousands of bloodthirsty vampires, I outed myself as a zombie.

The hall went silent.

The gawking vampires looked stunned and a bit confused.

'Everyone has a secret that makes them special. For some, like my friends, it's that they're unhuman, like us. For others, it's smaller things that make their life worth living. And as much as I want to rip their throats out and drink their blood, and man, I cannot tell you how much I want to do that, like all the time, I think of those secrets and keep my fangs tucked up in my gums. Everyone deserves their secrets – deserves to live.'

I squeezed Corina's hand and whispered, 'Can I say something?'

She nodded.

'Um, hi. Most people don't know you guys exist. I didn't until I got my zombie on and I met Corina. And she's amazing. She's like the coolest person ... well, vampire ... ever, and you're lucky to have her in your group, or tribe, or whatever you call your constitutionally protected right to assemble yourselves – although I somehow don't think the Founding Fathers would've sanctioned . . .'

I'd started to distract myself and needed to get back on track. 'Anyway, I know you guys think you're better than everyone else, and you know what? *You are.*

'Seriously, you live forever, you're super strong and you can fly. In my world, that pretty much makes you superheroes. And yet you're actually about to sacrifice, *kill*, a bunch of innocent people just to remind yourself how great you are?

'You might disagree about how innocent a telemarketer is, or someone who cuts you off in traffic, but that's not the point. The point is you *are* better than them. So, *act* better. *Be better.* You don't like they way do things, then stop hiding in your coffins and show them a *better* way. Teach them to be better, like you. Corina revealed herself to me, and I to her and now you, and I'm better for knowing her. Maybe what this country needs isn't fewer humans, but *more vampires.* Out in the open, being better than everyone else, and showing them how to be better.'

There was a murmur in the crowd.

Someone heckled, 'But we need to feed.'

'—so hungry—' muttered another.

I'd tried to appeal to their higher sense of self, but wondered if appealing to a lower need, their growling hunger, might enrol them in our face-off against camp evil. It was worth a try.

'Hey, Nesto,' I said. 'Why don't you tell them about Camp Nowannakidda.'

Nesto rose on his hind claws and shook the chupa off, returning to slimy boy form.

'I know what it's like to be hungry,' he said. 'I don't do human blood, but chicken heads, cows, squirrels – oh yeah, mmm-mmm, I love a good squirrel. But if you guys want to feed, why not eat people who eat people? And up in Canada, that country just north of us where all the bad weather comes from, there's this camp that captures kids to turn them into doughnuts.'

'So maybe instead of a sacrifice in Croxton,' I suggested, 'some of you might like to feast on the camp counsellors who held us captive?'

A sceptical murmur shot through the crowd. Some of the vampires licked their lips at the thought of eating the cannibals. Others shook their heads and tutted, clearly not believing Nesto's outlandish story.

'It's crazy but true,' said Corina. 'The camp is run by a flavour of evil that I'm sure you'll find delicious.'

I could see their pale eyes light up. The vampires *were* hungry, and we had a way to stop (or at the very least, relocate) tonight's sacrifice.

'I think we can help each other tonight,' I said.

'Yeah, come on!' said Corina. 'Who wants to raid Camp Cannibal?'

But the vamps weren't buying it. I half expected the crowd to explode into cheers and whoops. But they just stared at us.

'Should we try to make a getaway?' I asked.

'That won't be necessary,' replied a child's voice.

One tiny vampire, a little boy who looked no older than six, rose from the crowd into the air. The pint-sized vampire landed to share the stage with us. Corina lowered her head.

'What's wrong?' I said, thinking she was suddenly sad and maybe having second thoughts about killing off the cannibals.

'That's old man Konrad,' she said.

'Old man?' I scoffed. 'He's just a—'

'One of the elders,' said Corina.

'Old enough to have sailed over on the *Mayflower*,' the

boy spoke. His voice was high-pitched, young, but everyone in the hall hung on his words. 'And I would have died from dysentery on that voyage had a vampire not turned me, saving me from a watery grave. I've aged hundreds of years while watching this country, through a child's eyes, evolve from a colonial outpost to a superpower. Young Adam is right – as the superior species, we must lead by example, show these mere humans our true nobility.'

He took Corina's hand. 'Sister Corina has braved the stage, and risked her friends' lives to show us a way to save tonight's offerings from our hunger. Sister Corina, zombie Adam, and werecreature Nesto—'

'Chupacabra.'

'Count bless you,' Konrad said. 'Will the three of you lead us north?'

Corina nodded, and I said, 'We will.'

'Chu-pa-ca-bra,' said Ernesto. 'It's big in Latin America. Why has nobody heard of it?'

But to Nesto's frustration, nobody was listening.

'Mr Elder,' I said, tentatively.

'Yes?'

'Our friends and neighbours are trapped in the camp. So before you guys feast on the cannibal camp counsellors, would you help us free them?'

'It's the least we could do,' he said. 'They will not be harmed.'

Konrad turned to his flock of vampires and pressed his palms together. 'Go with Count's blessing.'

'Count's blessing go with thee,' they replied in unison.

28

In Which We Fly North

The hungry vamps assembled in the quad outside Convocation Hall and prepared for take-off.

'Corina,' I said, interrupting her as she received a constant stream of well-wishers. 'What about Nesto and me?'

'It's always about you, isn't it?' she said. I think the fame was going to her head. Either that or she was just being Corina.

She looked around the quad at the hundreds of vampires hovering just a foot or so off the ground and spotted a park bench. 'Hop on, boys,' she said.

I noticed a splat of bird poo on one side and decided that Nesto wouldn't mind too much. 'After you,' I said politely, gesturing to the poopy side of the bench.

He climbed on, perched up on his feet and I sat beside him, carefully avoiding any bird droppings.

'Hang on,' she said, 'be right back.'

I sat there with Nesto, watching the vampires milling around, just off the ground, chatting excitedly to each other in all sorts of languages I didn't understand.

When Corina returned, she wasn't alone. I nearly bounced off the bench.

'Hey, Adam,' said Crash, the guy I'd accidentally crushed to death a few weeks ago.

Awkward.

Crash looked much better than the last time I'd seen him, when Corina had saved him from human death (and thus saved me from being a murderer) and turned him into a vampire. He was paler now, with darker eyes. And he stood up straight, taller.

'Corina tells me I'm your ride,' he said.

'What do ya think?' Corina asked. 'Vampirism looks good on him, doesn't it?'

It really did.

Instead of his torn jeans and leather jacket, he wore a grey suit over a crisp white shirt. He looked more European cologne model than backstreet drug dealer. Though I wondered, *As a bloodsucker, is white really the best choice?* I was worried about his stain-removal strategy but decided to keep my laundry anxiety to myself. I simply said, 'Looking good, Crash.'

He grabbed the arm of the bench closer to me and Corina took the one near Nesto (and the bird poo) and they effortlessly lifted the bench into the air. At first my legs swung just a few feet off the ground, but then, as Konrad rose higher, the vampires followed him into the sky and we soared high above the university.

I sat back on the bench and gripped the wooden slats.

'Nervous flyer?' asked Crash.

'More like a nervous faller,' I said, since Park Bench Airways did not have any seatbelts.

'This is so chupamazing!' shouted Nesto. 'I can see my house from up here.'

He leaned over the back and hocked a big loogie* right onto his roof.

'*Really?*' I said.

'Yeah, c'mon, do your house, Adam, we're right above it.'

---

* For the unfamiliar, 'hocking a loogie' is like preparing and then dropping a saliva bomb. For the record, I do not approve.

I looked down and spotted my house. I was still mad at Mom and Dad for renting out our rooms and sending us away to camp, but I did miss them. They were on their way home, their second honeymoon cut short, and I wondered if they missed us. They said they were going to have some 'adult time', which is usually their term for emptying a bottle of wine once Amanda and I go to bed (I take out the recycling, reducing our household contribution to landfill and giving me an inside scoop on what's being consumed). I wasn't going to spit on our house, but I did notice the garden needed a good water.

'Mom's going to be sad if her flowers wilt,' I said. 'The vampires don't exactly have green thumbs.'

Nesto stood up on the bench and unzipped his shorts. He smirked at me with a devilish grin. 'If they need a watering, I could—'

'Do you want me to let go?' asked Corina.

Nesto sat back down.

'Good chupa,' she said.

Corina and Crash flew us higher, into the clouds. I felt the fine mist of the clouds whip against my decomposing skin.

Once we were above the clouds the vampire swarm picked up speed. I held on tight but Corina and Crash kept us steady. Not bound by roads, we flew north over the bright lights of Columbus and then over the eastern edge of Lake Erie.

'Hey look, guys,' I said, spotting below a massive plume of lit-up mist rise into the night sky. 'There's the Falls!'

The horseshoe-shaped waterfall was pink, and then green. As we soared high above one of the wonders of the world, the water was illuminated with every colour of the rainbow. It was mesmerising, and for a brief moment I forgot all about vampires and cannibals and doughnuts, and watched as the colourful water rushed over a hidden cliff, as it had probably done since the days of the dinosaurs.

Poor dinosaurs, I thought, suddenly remembering I was flying with a flock of vampires.

'Can you believe we actually did that?' said Nesto. 'That was so cool.'

Now that I was safely out of the tin can and flying over the mighty Niagara Falls, it was cool. That's what I loved about my friends – we did crazy, daring things, things that before, all by myself, I'd have been too scared to even dream about. But we did them.

Together.

We cut the corner of Lake Ontario and pushed north of the suburban sprawl that hugged the lake's shore. Finally, as we flew over the great expanse of dark wilderness below, the sky was lit only by the twinkling galaxy above.

I tilted my head back and gaped at the constellations. I felt my stomach rise as we began our descent into Camp Nowannakidda airspace.

'Better close your mouth, Adam,' said Crash. 'It's one of the little tricks you learn the hard way when you start flying.'

'Good point,' I said, shutting my fly trapper. I was not interested in ingesting any insects.

Finally, we flew over the fenced-in camp. The vampires descended in the main field in front of the mess hall. All of the campers were tucked up in their tents and as we silently touched down, with not so much as a bump, I might add, I heard the camp counsellors in the dining hall talking and laughing.

I nudged Corina and pointed. 'They're in there,' I whispered.

Corina found Konrad and lowered her head in respect. 'My elder, that's an all-you-can-eat buffet in there.'

The childlike vampire elder grinned a predator's grin. 'Why don't you introduce us?'

Corina looked at Nesto and I. 'Come on guys, let's say hello and goodbye.'

As we approached the door, I heard old Mrs Lebkuchen: 'You've done well, my children. This year's batch may be our best yet. The campers are getting fatter, tastier.'

Corina pushed open the door. Mrs Lebkuchen stood, hunched on her cane, talking to the dozen camp counsellors who were spread around three small tables, stuffing themselves on boxes of Can Nibble doughnuts.

Mrs Lebkuchen noticed me and narrowed her sunken eyes. '*Healthier*, I mean.'

The camp staff all turned to see me standing at the doorway.

'Um, Adam,' said Growl, 'the mess hall's off limits to campers after dinner, you should be—'

'Save it, Growl. I know what you cannibals are really up to – fattening us up so you can donutify us. Which is really disgusting, by the way.'

They laughed.

'You're acting crazy, Adam,' said Growl.

'And *crazy* is rescuing your ingredients,' I said.

'Yeah, you and what army?' asked Duke.

'You probably didn't want to ask that,' I said, stepping aside.

Konrad walked through the door and inhaled. He took a big breath in through his nose and closed his eyes, savouring the smell.

'We thank you, Count,' he began, 'for what we are about to receive. For this bountifully place filled with humans who eat humans.'

Mrs Lebkuchen raised her cane at me. 'You cannot stop us. There will always be children who wander into the woods, happy to eat our food . . . to *become* our food. And people always look the other way.'

'You're about to wish we never wandered into your woods,' said Corina, turning to leave.

I held Mrs Lebkuchen's gaze. 'And I'm not looking away,' I said. 'I'm looking right at you, and I see pure evil.'

Nesto and I followed Corina out of the door as the waiting vampires filed past us, storming the dining hall for their midnight feast.

We heard screams as the vampires finally got their sacrifice. Corina stood beside me, listening to the howls of horror coming from inside.

I turned to her, transfixed by the sound of the killing, and asked, 'You don't want to join in?'

'I do, but I won't,' she said. 'I want to feed, but I'm going to keep it in check.'

'We can always stop for doughnuts on the way home,' I half-joked to try to get a smile from her.

'Don't tempt me,' she said, suppressing a grin.

'Wouldn't dream of it,' I said. 'But we should get home.'

'Do we have to?' whined Nesto. 'I want to say "Hi" and "Bye" to somebody first.'

'A certain weremoose?' asked Corina.

'Maybe.'

'Go find her,' I said.

Nesto jumped down onto all fours and let out a howl. Within seconds, he'd transformed back into his slimy chupa self. He howled again.

From the trees, a moose call answered back.

29

In Which We Get Our Camp On

Corina and I arrived at the tents where the kids were sleeping. They had no idea that in just a few days they would have become tasty pastries.

'Should we tell them?' I asked.

'Would they believe us?'

'I'm still not sure I believe it,' I said. But that wasn't true. After facing down zealous zombees and cannibalistic camp counsellors, I was starting to think that there was nothing in the world that could surprise me any more.

And then I felt something wet on my cheek.

Corina had kissed me.

'Thanks for believing in me,' she said. 'At the convention.'

I touched my cheek, the sensation of the kiss slowly disappearing, and wrestled with a moral dilemma.

Should I ever wash it again? But of course, there was really no question – *hygiene first*.

'You believed in yourself,' I said. 'And I don't care what your parents say, everyone listened to you.'

'You're a good friend, Adam,' she said.

Oh come on! Seriously, I thought. *Still in the friend zone?*

Another howl broke the night-time sound of crickets. Corina pulled me past the tents, towards the treeline. I was hopeful for another kiss, but it wasn't to be.

'Shhhh,' she said, grabbing hold of me and flying us up into the trees.

She popped us onto a branch (I was getting used to this) and pointed down. 'Now isn't that cute?'

Below our dangling feet, our friend, the scaly chupacabra, rubbed noses with Melissa the weremoose. Nesto howled gently and she answered back with her trumpet call.

Corina and I giggled.

'I know you're up there!' called Nesto. 'I have enhanced hearing, you know!'

'Are you two making out?' shouted Melissa the moose. 'Aren't they cute, Nesty?'

'This is madness,' grunted Corina. She grabbed me and we descended in a controlled plummet.

'Hi, Nesto,' I said. 'Hi, Melissa.'

'Honestly.' The moose laughed. 'I think you three can't be away from each other for, like, five seconds.'

'We're a pretty good team,' I said.

'I'd say,' she said. 'You flew in a bunch of vampires to take out that old witch and her minions. She's been haunting these woods since my grandmoose was just a calf.'

'I don't think you and your herd will have to worry about them any more,' I said.

'Cannibals out, vampires in,' Melissa snorted.

'She's got a point,' said Corina.

'Of course I've got a point, I always have a point,' Melissa bellowed.

'I like her, *Nesty*,' said Corina.

'So do I,' he replied.

'Melissa, can I ask you a favour?' I said.

'I'm not introducing you to my sister,' she said. 'I think you're taken.' Melissa nudged her head against the fence at Corina.

'Gross,' said Corina.

'Okay, maybe I will,' quipped Melissa.

With my unbeating heart well and truly crushed, I asked Melissa if she and her father and the rest of the herd would keep their eyes open and antlers fixed on the visiting vampires. 'I don't know if any of them intend to stay,' I said, 'but it'd be great if they didn't extend their feast to include the entire country.'

'Think it serves them right,' said Melissa. 'The whole country's been chomping on children for years. Gobbling up their doughnuts and keeping this place going.'

'She *does* have a point,' agreed Corina. 'Maybe the vampires should stay – take their sacrifice on the people. Every doughnut dipper up here is guilty.'

'But they didn't know,' I said.

'They didn't ask,' said Melissa. 'They're totally complicit.'

I thought hard about this – it made my brain hurt. Did she have a point? Everyone was happily eating doughnuts made from people and nobody bothered to ask where the deliciousness actually came from. My dad had always said that 'ignorance was no excuse', but I wondered if ignorance *of ignorance* was. Did they even know how ignorant they were?

Maybe instead of unleashing a swarm of vampires on these cannibals of convenience, it would be a lot better to expose the truth.

'We're going to stay,' I said.

'Yay!' shouted Ernesto.

'We are?' asked Corina.

'Yep, we've got the camp to ourselves for nearly two more weeks and we can make sure everyone knows what was really happening here.'

'And we can help,' said a woman's voice from the darkness. It was Corina's mom.

'Are you spying on me?' Corina asked.

'We were looking for you,' said her dad, his one hand holding her mother's. 'We wanted to apologise.'

Nesto whispered to Melissa. 'I didn't know vampires knew how to do that.'

'You made us very proud tonight, Corina,' said Mrs Parker. 'It was very brave. And I haven't been very—'

'Nice,' said Corina.

'Understanding,' she said. 'It's hard ...'

'Living with you, sure is,' snapped Corina.

'I didn't want this life for you, and I suppose it's easier to ignore you than to face up to the fact that you're inheriting a life neither of us wanted. Your father and

I were made vampires – we weren't born this way. We didn't even want children—'

'Thanks,' sniffled Corina. I tried to put my arm around her, but she shoved me off.

'Corina, we love you,' her mother said. 'We just never wanted this kind of life for you. You're our beautiful baby girl, and it kills us a little bit every day that you're growing into the monster that we've become.'

'I'm just me, Mom,' said Corina.

'You showed us that tonight,' said Dr Parker. 'Like Adam said, you showed us that you're *better* – better than us, and better than our fears of what you'd become.'

He reached out his one arm and drew Corina into a hug. Corina let her mom in too, until all three Parkers were squeezed tight like a vampire triple-pack.

'We have something to show you,' said Mrs Parker. 'Children, you may all wish to see this. Especially you, Adam.'

Corina's parents led us back towards the mess hall. Melissa came too after Corina hopped the fence and carried her back over, in a pretty girl form.

'I'm fairly sure I don't need to see this,' I said, as we approached the scene of the vampire sacrifice.

Elder Konrad was waiting at the door, his hands

folded neatly in front of him. 'There they are,' he said. 'The three brave souls who stood up to our kind. And who is this? A female werewolf.'

'Moose,' said Melissa. 'Werewolves are wimps. Moose are mega.'

'Indeed.' Konrad laughed, gesturing to the door. 'If you please.'

I stepped in reluctantly, expecting to see hollowed-out bodies, guts on the floor, and the wood timbers of the building spray-painted in blood. But instead we found our captors on their knees, hands tied behind their backs.

'You didn't . . . *sacrifice* them?' I asked.

'We sure scared them, but we exercised restraint,' Konrad said, looking at Corina. 'We tried to be a bit *better* than our usual selves.'

'But they're evil,' said Corina.

'And they'll be punished,' said Mrs Parker.

'Once *you* call the police to arrest them,' said Dr Parker.

'I know just who to call,' said Corina, pulling Officer Bobert Campbell's card out of her pocket. She looked at me sternly, but a smile won out. 'Just no more show tunes.'

'I can't make that promise,' I teased.

Konrad approached Corina and said, 'You've given us a lot to think about. You'd make a great elder one day, Corina Parker.'

'Maybe one day,' she said. 'But right now I want to hang out with my friends. Oh, and get these cannibals busted.'

'That's my girl,' said Mrs Parker.

Konrad walked slowly out of the mess hall and rounded up his flock. He rose into the air and the vampires followed him into the night sky. The swarm of bloodsuckers clouded out the stars and disappeared to the south, leaving us to our summer camp.

'We'll guard them,' said Dr Parker. 'You kids deserve some fun tonight.'

'I have just the idea,' I said, zipping into the kitchen and finding graham crackers, bars of chocolate and marshmallows. 'Who's hungry for s'mores?'

The four of us – a zombie, a vampire, a chupacabra and a weremoose – walked down to the lakefront and built a fire. And finally just ... hung out with nothing to worry about.

Epilogue

In Which We Drive Home

It turned out that Officer Bobert Campbell knew a guy in the Royal Canadian Mounted Police (they had vacationed together once, though not in 'Nam) and after Corina called him, he called in the Mounties.

I was disappointed that they didn't ride in mounted on horses, but they did show up pretty sharpish in black sedans with flashing lights. They arrested all of the camp counsellors including that old witch Mrs Lebkuchen, who shouted madly in her defence that she really was a witch and that eating children was part of her religion.

With our captors gone, and Corina's parents as the camp's new chaperones, we had a campfire every night. One night, we took turns telling ghost stories. Corina told a story of a sect of vampires planning a mass sacrifice and I recounted what Amanda called 'a preposterous tale' of the camp that was actually a fattening pen for people.

When the news finally broke about what became known as Camp Cannibal, the rest of the parents, including mine, all drove up to collect us kids and take us home.

On the drive back (completely devoid of show tunes), I noticed that all of the Can Nibble doughnut shops had closed. Those Mounties sure had moved quickly – I was impressed. But outside one shuttered doughnut shop, I spotted a sign that read: 'Coming Soon: Another Mighty Mooseburger Shack.'

Will people never learn, I wondered.

That night, after a celebratory falafel* pizza (thanks Dad!), I met up with Nesto and Corina in the backyard. Adamini buzzed around, apparently happy to have us back.

'What are we going to do with the rest of the summer?' I asked.

'Actually,' said Corina, 'Amanda and I are going to hang out tomorrow.'

* I thought that in honour of Corina, I'd give the meatballs a rest for a while.

What?

I'd faced down cannibals and stopped a vampocalypse, but Corina becoming friends with my sister was more horrible than anything I could imagine.

The End

Acknowledgements

As ever, I need to thank my awesome wife, Sidonie, for her support and encouragement to bring this character to life. Adam Meltzer would've remained an idea in my head (or at least a corpse in the ground!) had she not laughed out loud at the first few pages of my very first draft.

It's been such a great pleasure to get out from behind the writing desk and go into schools and meet the dedicated teachers and librarians who champion reading for our young people. All writers owe a huge debt to these unsung heroes of our society. If I could hug them all, I would.

I also want to thank the team at Faber Children's for not only introducing Adam Meltzer to the world in the first place but for publishing this sequel which probably breaks all the rules of children's books. Leah Thaxton and Rebecca Lewis-Oakes edited Adam's musings with grace and skill, and Hannah Love has sung his praises so that his tale can be told far and wide. In my mind, Adam's stories are not so much *for* kids, as they are about being a kid. I can remember being Adam's age very clearly, and it's my creative ambition to channel that still-forming point of view in these books. The world is a complex and confusing place, and Adam is trying his best to navigate through it. He and his friends don't always get it right, but they're trying their best.

Lastly, this book is dedicated to my parents who, unlike Adam's mom and dad, never kicked me out, rented out my room, or signed a release form they didn't fully read . . .

. . . not that I know of.

Dear Reader,

There's a sequence in the book that's drawn from an image I saw as a boy. I visited the Holocaust Centre in Toronto on a school trip and was shaken and horrified by the pictures I saw and the stories I heard.

It still haunts me. And as the world becomes more complex, all of us need to be on guard against horrors of the past becoming a reality in our present. As Adam's dad instructs him, 'ignorance is no excuse'.

Chances are, if you're reading this, there is a Holocaust museum or education centre near you. I urge you to visit.

Yours truly,
Jeff
London, March 2015

It's 1945 in Germany, and Hanno and Effi are on the run.

An exceptional tale of courage, ingenuity, and the remarkable bonds
formed during wartime.

Winner – Costa Children's Book Award

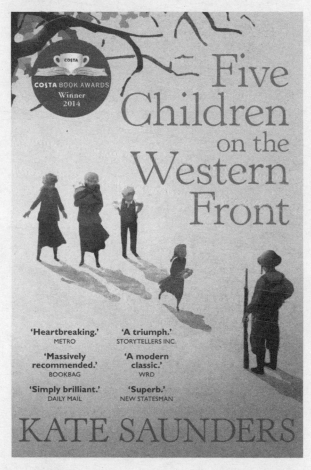

COSTA BOOK AWARDS
Winner
2014

Five
Children
on the
Western
Front

'Heartbreaking.'
METRO

'A triumph.'
STORYTELLERS INC.

'Massively
recommended.'
BOOKBAG

'A modern
classic.'
WRD

'Simply brilliant.'
DAILY MAIL

'Superb.'
NEW STATESMAN

KATE SAUNDERS

It's the eve of the First World War.

An incredible, heart-wrenching sequel to E. Nesbit's
Five Children and It. The children have all grown up – war will
change their lives for ever.

CONFIDENTIAL
-TOP SECRET-

THE SPY'S
HANDBOOK

HERBIE BRENNAN

spy files enclosed
read with caution

ff

The complete guide to professional spying!

Whether you're just a bit nosy, or you want to launch a full-scale investigation into your neighbours, this indispensable handbook will teach you everything you need to know, from codes, ciphers, invisible ink and signalling to guidance on drops and safe houses.

Faber Children's Classics

Faber Children's Classics